ISBN- 978-0-578-83442-9

"Men have more teeth than women. The female is, as it were, a mutilated male. Females are weaker and colder in nature. Compared to men, women are immature, deficient, deformed. They are even a bit monstrous. Men have hotter blood than women, a more important role in reproduction, and are generally more perfect. "

–Aristotle

The Company Men

Written and Illustrated by Coyote Paria

The Company Men

Table of Contents:

Part 1: Good Morning, Manazonia

<u>1</u>

It was said that no man could resist Conrad Ryder. He was a little over seven feet tall, handsome and muscular like a bull, with shoulders like a tank, sturdy, square, and broad. Conrad was a natural blond, with squinting cobalt blue eyes and teeth that seemed to be larger, whiter and more square than ordinary teeth. He walked with a sort of cocky nonchalance, gloating his invincibility with every confident thud of his massive boots.

Conrad flashed the bartender, a sideways grin. The bartender, who was around the same age as Conrad (25 or so), ruddy, and dark haired, smiled back unsurely. The bar was dark except for a few neon lights advertising different brands of liquor. It was filled with only men.

"You're The Company Man, aren't you?" the bartender asked darkly. "I've heard about you."

Conrad laughed. It was a deep, throaty laugh that made his large Adam's apple quiver in his thick neck. He slammed a few bills against the glass counter between himself and the bartender. The bartender jumped as though expecting Conrad to hit him.

"You have, have you?" Conrad replied, grinning. His voice was very deep and booming. He paused and then added "Beer please," as an after thought. The bartender grabbed a glass from under the counter and poured him a beer from the tap.

"Yea, you're the guy that took out that beast from the Strange Lands, cut out its eye with a knife," said the bartender.

"Yup," confirmed Conrad. "I still have the eye in my apartment. It's as big as my couch. I think it's starting to rot though," he paused to lift the mug of beer to his lips and gulp it down. "Because it smells like crap now."

"Don't you think you should get rid of it?," the bartender asked.

Conrad shook his head.

"Nah."

"I hear that your partner was killed in that battle," said the bartender.

"He was," said Conrad. He slammed a few more bills down on the counter. "Another beer."

The bartender filled another mug with beer and slid it across the table toward Conrad. Conrad caught it with one massive hand.

"I'm sorry," the bartender commiserated.

"Don't be," said Conrad indifferently. He

lifted the mug off of the counter and drank down its contents in two gulps. "We weren't close."

"But I heard..."

"Forget what you've heard. I've moved on," interrupted Conrad disparagingly. He started counting the fingers on one hand and then added cheerfully. "I'll need like, I don't know. Like seven more beers."

2

It took a lot of alcohol to get Conrad buzzed, he was large, and tall, and muscled like a tank and could usually drink beer like it was water without feeling any real effect from it. He drank at home, he drank at work. He drank alone, he drank with friends. He drank when people could see him and when people couldn't see him. On the bus, in his car while he was driving, while he was talking to his boss, and on the toilet sometimes, when taking a shit grew tiresome and he needed something to entertain himself. It was rare to catch him without a beer in his hand and today was no exception. Conrad lifted a can of beer to his parted lips and took a deep slow drag from it. Today his hair was spiky and over-gelled and his broad chin was bristly with unshaven blond whiskers. He wore cammo pants, large brown boots, a black sleeveless shirt, a denim jacket emblazoned with the insignia of his country's embassy, and a red bandana like a headband around his forehead. The loops of his belt held an assortment of knives guns and grenades.

The government building where Conrad worked (known as "The Company"), was a large, square, glass building that, from a distance, resembled an ice cube. The insignia of The Company, a large, silver, five-pointed star with a circle around it, emblazoned the building's two, large tall front doors. Conrad ascended the steep marble steps to the embassy's front doors and pushed through them, entering the building. Employees of the government walked to-and-fro across the marble floor, carrying documents; discussing business with each other. Most were dressed more professionally than Conrad with dark blue slacks and button down shirts. All were men.

Conrad walked past the large, marble fountain, at the center of the embassy lobby, and toward a door in the back where he knew the company meeting room was. He was supposed to be assigned a new mission and a new partner today. Conrad entered the room. An old man named Weston was in there, talking loudly and gesturing aggressively toward the projector screen at the front of the room. There was some kind of a chart or graph up there.

"Is your mission understood?" Weston asked the six young men, sitting in a row, behind a long desk, facing the projector screen.

"Yes, sir. It is," replied the row of young men gruffly and more or less in unison. They all rose and exited the room, walking past Conrad, who took another swig from the can of beer, and belched aggressively in Weston's direction.

"You're late, Conrad," Weston growled, not sounding at all surprised. The old man was tall and slender with thinning grey hair that stood on end. His voice was harsh and abrupt. Conrad was a foot taller than him and not intimidated.

"Yea, so what?" replied Conrad. "Just tell me what you told them but without all of your stupid graphs."

Weston sighed and shook his head.

"You know kid, I'd fire you if your dad wasn't my boss," said Weston. "...And your other dad wasn't my *other* boss."

"Yea, yea, just get on with it," said Conrad

dismissively.

Weston sighed again. He clicked a key on his computer and the graph on the projector screen was replaced by a detailed drawing of a naked person. Conrad glanced up at it, his mouth falling open in amazement.

"What on Earth...." Conrad murmured. He had seen plenty of naked people in his lifetime but never one that looked like this. This person had thick freakish thighs, and a slit between its legs where its penis should have been. There were a couple of large, round protrusions jutting out from its chest and its hair was very long, down to its waist. Its arms and legs were drawn spread-eagle and a number of notations and measurements were scribbled around it.

"What indeed," said Weston, amused by Conrad's confusion. "Only higher ranking officials know about these things."

"What kind of a man is this?" Conrad asked.

"It's not a man," said Weston.

"If it's not a man then what is it?" Conrad murmured with amazement. The strange creature truly perplexed him, not because he had never seen strange creatures before. He certainly had. But because this one looked so much like a human.

Conrad blinked. "It must be some kind of a...a *shman*," he said.

"That's right, Conrad. Its a *shman*,"

confirmed Weston. "An incubator that can walk like a man. When a man is born with the *shman* deformities, he must be circumcised and removed from society, for the safety of the public."

"It has a butt on its chest. Does it poop out of its chest hole?" Conrad asked.

"Conrad, are you *drunk*?"

"Maybe."

"Anyway, we can't have live shmen walking around with their heads and limbs intact," explained Weston.

"Why not?"

Weston snatched the beer out of Conrad's hand before he knew what was happening.

"*Hey*," Conrad complained.

"Because, we have a treaty with The Overlords, Conrad," said Weston, as though he were explaining this to an exceptionally stupid child. "They have it up their ass that prophecies are a thing, so if we let a live shman walk around. If the Overlords find out about this before we take care of it, they'll blow our society off the map! Everything. Will. Die. Do you understand?   important that you take this seriously!   If you've never taken anything seriously in your life, take this seriously."

"Ok, *ok*, I'm taking it seriously," groaned Conrad. "So what's the mission?"

Weston clicked a key on his computer and the drawing of the shman was replaced by a blurry photograph of a person with long sunflower yellow hair, a smooth, pointed chin, and pouty lips painted red. It wore a knee-length, pink shirt with no sleeves and a ruffle along the bottom of it. There were no pants underneath, only bear, hairless legs and a pair of very strange and impractical looking shoes.

"A live shman was spotted in the Strange Lands. He...I'm sorry, grammatically I think you're supposed to say *she*..."

"Pht. Grammar," Conrad interjected indifferently.

"Well anyway...*she* is thought to be the same shman reported as still born twenty-one years ago, whose embryo was never recovered. Your mission is to track it down and kill it."

"Whatever, that'll be easy," said Conrad.

"Give me my beer back."

"Not as easy as you think, Conrad. It's been reported that a group of men are protecting the shman, powerful mercenaries. They've already killed three of my agents."

"Still easy," grunted Conrad dismissively. "I want my beer back."

Weston walked to the dumpster in the corner of the room and poured the remaining contents of the can into it.

"Take this seriously," said Weston.

"I told you I am taking this seriously....you crusty old ball sack," mumbled Conrad.

"And to make sure you *are* taking this seriously, I've arranged for your new partner to be Jerry Cosco."

Conrad groaned loudly.

"Come on, man. *Jerry Cosco*? Everybody hates Jerry Cosco. He's the worst," said Conrad.

"Have you even met Jerry Cosco?" asked Weston with irritation.

"No."

"So why are you so down on him? What do you even know about Jerry Cosco?"

"I know that he's the worst," grumbled Conrad.

Weston sighed and shook his head.

"I won't lie to you, its true that Jerry's not a great fighter but that boy's got a good head on his shoulders....and unlike you, he *does* take this seriously. I assigned him as your partner because together the two of you might make two halves of one decent agent."

"Well I guess I don't have a choice," growled Conrad.

Weston walked over to an intercom built into one of the walls of the room. He pushed a button on the machine and spoke in into its plastic grid speaker.

"Dan, send Jerry Cosco down here," Weston said to the man on the other end of the intercom.

"You got it, boss," the intercom barked back.

A few moments passed and then the door to the meeting room creaked open. A short, wiry man with conservative brown hair, and large square thick-framed glasses shuffled into the room. His expression was that of a professional bringer of bad news, grim and joyless, but professionally so, that is to say, with a sort of an empty, dead, detachedness.

"Conrad this is Jerry," said Weston, pointing to the shorter of the two men. He pointed back at Conrad and added. "Jerry, Conrad."

"Nice to meet you," Jerry said without smiling. He spoke in a dry, flat monotone.

"Uh huh," said Conrad somewhat disingenuously.

"Jerry has been working in our clerical and administrative department for three years now and has just been promoted to a rank 15."

"Shit. He out ranks me?" Conrad swore. He had never partnered with an agent who had a higher rank than him and didn't very much like the idea of it.

Jerry ignored this comment with all of the patience and enthusiasm of a rotting piece of drift wood. He stuck his hand out for Conrad to shake.

"I look forward to working with you," Jerry said, still frowning.

Conrad grabbed Jerry's small, bony hand in his comparatively massive one and shook it aggressively. Jerry's whole arm was wrenched rapidly upward and downward and he stumbled forward awkwardly, his dark eyes, which were strangely magnified by his thick bifocals, grew wide and nervous with his discomfort. Conrad released Jerry's hand and he drew it back quickly.

"Yea, right back at'cha," said Conrad.

<u>3</u>

Jerry was quiet for a long time, sitting in the passenger seat of Conrad's red convertible. He was holding the stack of documents he had with him in a white-knuckled death grip to stop them from flying away as Conrad sped over the suspension bridge leading into the city.

"Can you please, put the top back up on the damn car," Jerry complained after awhile.

"There's no top on this car," lied Conrad. "It got ripped off by a thing somehow."

"Oh. Ok," said Jerry.

A few more moments passed, during which time both men remained silent. Conrad sped past a few slow moving cars, the tires of his car squealed as he gave the wheel a sharp tug and passed them on the right. They drove past a pawn shop, a hunting supply store, a burger joint, and a strip club with the words "Guys! Guys! Guys!" lit up in bright, fuchsia, cursive, neon letters. There were men on the sidewalks, men on the cross walks, men in the cars, and men looking out of the windows of office buildings over head. There were pairs of elderly men who walked hand and hand, accompanied by their families of male children. A sexy, muscular, and scantily-clad man lay sprawled seductively on a billboard advertising a soft drink in a red can.

Conrad's convertible slowed to a stop behind a large black truck that was stopped at a red light. Jerry took the opportunity to open one of his folders and quickly ruffle through it.

"It seems direct information about the shman is very illusive," reported Jerry dutifully. "It has not been discovered by The Company *how* she was able to escape Mantropolis, for *how long* she has been hiding in the Strange Lands, or *how* she recruited her mercenary followers."

"Uh huh," said Conrad. "What's with all this herm and she stuff? Could you just call it a he. It's less confusing."

"'Her is the correct grammar," explained Jerry.

"Yea, I don't have time for all of this pretentious grammar that became obsolete 500 years ago. Just call it a he so that I know what you're talking about," said Conrad.

Jerry groaned and shook his head.

"Ok fine. What *is* known about *him*, however, are the names and prior residences of his followers. Pictures of their faces where taken by the first team of Company Men who were killed trying to exterminate the shman," said Jerry.

"You don't say?"

"Their body cameras were destroyed with their bodies but before that, the pictures were digitally uploaded to headquarters," said Jerry. He flipped through the papers in the folder on his lap and saw five or six blurry photographs of large muscular men with rifles, standing protectively around an elegant, slender woman with long, sunflower yellow hair.

"From the pictures, experts were able to identify three of the shman's followers," said Jerry.

"What makes you think they're followers? Maybe they just stole him," said Conrad.

"Good point," said Jerry. "Anyway, the three men identified were Arnold Copperfield, Sidney Morrison and Tommy Higgenmier. Morrison, worked in a pawnshop on the corner of Viel and 5th street. He lived with one of his fathers not to far from there...and um....Copperfield was a construction worker.

His apartment is in Boroughs Town. Higgenmier worked at the strip club—"

Conrad interrupted him:

"Strip club? We're going there first."

"Um ok," said Jerry. "It's the one on the other side of the city, though. So it might make more sense to hit some of the closer locations first. Like Boroughs Town. That's literally 30 seconds away," He paused and pointed at a green traffic sign with the words Boroughs Town printed on it in white letters. "See it's right over there."

"Don't care," said Conrad as he watched the red traffic light turn green and the black truck in front of him rev its engine and speed off into the distance. "We're going to the strip club."

"The strip clubs a half an hour away," said Jerry.

"Uh, *yea* but it's a strip club," said Conrad as though this were the most obvious thing in the world. He lifted a can of bear out of the drink holder between himself and Jerry, then, popped the tab, lifted it to his parted lips, and gulped it down. "That other shit you were talking about is lame."

"Uh...put the beer down when you're driving maybe?" said Jerry, eyeing the pavement nervously as Conrad drifted into the next lane, then swerved, narrowly avoiding an oncoming sports car. The man in the sports car shouted profanities and smashed his fist down on the car horn.

"Yea, fuck you too, buddy!" Conrad screamed, taking both of his hands off of the wheel to flash the offending driver both of his middle fingers. The car swerved into the other lane again and Jerry grabbed the wheel to steady it.

"Holy shit! Holy shit! Holy shit!" Jerry swore as he leaned over the driver's side seat and gripped the wheel, hyperventilating. "What the hell is wrong with you?"

Conrad put his hands back on the wheel and continued speeding down the road.

"Nothing," he said calmly, almost sounding confused. It was as though his previous outburst had never happened. "Why are you so worked up?"

"Why am I so worked up?" Jerry repeated incredulously. He was still hyperventilating, clutching the stack of folders with white, bloodless fingers.

"Yea, that's what I just asked," said Conrad.

"Shit dude, I'm worked up because you tried to kill me," said Jerry incredulously.

"Well, shit, dude, if I wanted to kill you. You'd be dead, bro," said Conrad, grinning. Then he laughed a deep booming laugh. "Don't your ever pick a fight with some dude you don't know just for the hell of it?"

"This. No. Don't do that again," said Jerry.

"Do what?"

"Pick a fight with a dude you don't know," said Jerry. "We're getting off task."

"So when's the last time you've been laid, boy?" asked Conrad conversationally.

"*That comment*," growled Jerry angrily. "Is *off task*."

"Because it seems to be like you need to get laid," continued Conrad.

"Off task," Jerry snapped again.

A few minutes passed. The two men were silent. Conrad's convertible weaved between speeding cars and Jerry clutched his folders like they would stop him from dying if they crashed.

"Can I ask you something?" Conrad inquired conversationally as he continued driving.

"What?" asked Jerry.

"How many wieners can you stick in your mouth?" asked Conrad.

"Conrad, do I have to point out that that comment about the wieners in my mouth is *off task*?"

"Eh, you're no fun," said Conrad.

"Let's agree right now to have no conversations irrelevant to the mission," said Jerry. "I will not have this mission be sabotaged by unnecessary distractions."

Jerry stopped talking abruptly as the car jerked to a stop.

Conrad parked the red convertible in a space outside of a building with a giant neon sign, depicting a buff man in a g-string and a cowboy hat sprawled seductively over the words "The Rodeo." A line of excited men—young and old, short and tall, fat and skinny—stood outside, waiting to get in.

Conrad and Jerry got out of the car and walked inside. A burly black bouncer holding a clip board stopped them before they could walk through the door.

"You, the big guy," the bouncer said, pointing to Conrad. "You can go in."

Conrad walked through the door and disappeared into the crowded club. Jerry followed. The bouncer put his hand out to block Jerry from the entrance. Jerry took a nervous step backward.

"You," boomed the bouncer, pointing to Jerry. "You're not on the list."

The bouncer shook his head and tapped the blank piece of paper on his clipboard with his index finger.

"No, no you don't understand," laughed Jerry nervously, shaking his head. "We're not here to see the boys. We're Company Men on official business."

Jerry removed his wallet from his back pocket and opened it so that his Company ID card was visible.

"Oh, I see," said the bouncer. "You must be here about Higgenmier."

"Uh...yes, actually," said Jerry. "Did you know him?"

"Sure, he was a stripper here," said the bouncer. "Used to talk to me about weird shit all the time."

"Did he show any interest in the shman folklore?" Jerry asked.

"Uh huh," said the bouncer. "The dude was obsessed with it."

"Really, how so?" Jerry inquired.

"Well, for one thing, he'd be talking about it whenever I saw him. He was all *woman born of woman will slay the Overlords* this and *I want to stick my dick in their crotch holes that*. It's really not all that surprising that he's in trouble with The Company. Frankly I'm surprised it's taken this long. Is that why he disappeared? Because he's on the run from The Company?"

"I'm not at liberty to divulge that information," replied Jerry stiffly.

"Man, that boy was weird," said the bouncer, shaking his head. "I knew it was just a matter of time."

"What specifically, did Higgenmier tell you about shmen?" Jerry probed.

"Well, I told him I wasn't interested. But he seemed to want to tell people about them, like a public service announcement, and I told him that that would get him in trouble with The Company, but he wouldn't listen," said the bouncer. "He'd be talking about how he wanted to have sex with a shman and sometimes, he would give out this illegal pornography from the before times. But that's about it. There's not much more to tell."

"This illegal pornography, did you ever see any of it?" Jerry asked.

"Yea it was like, pages ripped out of old magazines. Pictures of naked shmen," said The bouncer. "He thought they were sexy."

"Heh. Imagine that," Jerry mused, biting his lip nervously.

"I don't know why, though. I think they're just weird looking," said the bouncer.

"Yea," agreed Jerry. "They're gross. Listen, did you ever receive any of these illegal pictures from Mr. Higgenmier?"

"Yea, he tried to give me one before he disappeared. I told him I wasn't interested in it but he insisted. So I just, you know, smiled at him, and then threw it in the trash after he walked away. It's probably still in that trash can over there," said the bouncer, pointing at a dumpster near the back entrance of the club. "If you want it for evidence or whatever."

4

After what felt like hours of digging through the trash, Jerry entered the strip club, his dirt-caked fingernails gripped a crumpled piece of paper. A used condom from the trash can was stuck in his disheveled hair and his blue suit jacket was streaked with grime.

Jerry spotted Conrad, with a beer in his hand, getting a lap dance from a muscular man with wavy red hair. Jerry stalked over toward him, glaring. Conrad didn't notice. All of his attention was focused on the young man's g-string clad ass gyrating in his face.

"Conrad," Jerry growled with irritation. "Conrad! Remember the thing we talked about?"

"About how many penises you can fit in your mouth?" Conrad asked, without taking his eyes off of the gyrating stripper in his lap.

"No Conrad, the thing I said about being *off task*," growled Jerry.

"Huh?" said Conrad, still watching the gyrating stripper in his lap.

"This is important," said Jerry.

"Later," grunted Conrad dismissively.

"Conrad, I have a lead." Jerry said.

This time Jerry was ignored completely.

"Hey, *hey!*" Jerry said again, waving his

arms to get Conrad's attention.

Again, he was ignored. Frustrated, Jerry retreated to a chair in the corner of the dark, crowded room and watched the clock on the wall, above the black-lit bar. The minute hand on that clock moved like a hard turd moves out of a tight asshole. 10 minutes passed. It felt like ten thousand years. Jerry thought about how much he just wanted to get this stupid job over with so that he could go home and eat the left over pasta in his refrigerator. He tore his eyes away from the clock and glanced back over at Conrad. Conrad was still getting a lap dance from the same stripper. Jerry glanced back at the clock. Half an hour had passed. It might as well have been 15 thousand years. Jerry glanced back over at Conrad. Now Condrad was making out with the stripper. Jerry crossed his arms and slouched forward in his chair. Time passed. Jerry stopped keeping track of it. He entertained himself by thinking about how bored and hungry he was. That leftover pasta at home in his refrigerator seemed to speak to him telepathically now. *Come to me, Jerry. I'm waiting for you. These shitty slutty fuckers. They don't understand real love. They'll never have what we have.* Jerry glanced back over at Conrad. Conrad was downing what must have been his seventh beer while the red-headed stripper gyrated his g-string clad crotch.

Jerry stood up and stormed over to the stripper, glowering.

"You," snapped Jerry, pointing to the stripper. "Get the fuck off of him. We have important business to discuss."

The stripper stood up and turned toward Jerry, glaring.

"Hey, man, fuck you. If you want to talk to me like that, I can knock your fuckin' teeth out. Would you like that, huh? You little piece of shit. I bet your dick is two inches long." snapped the stripper.

"I said get lost, you stupid whore!" yelled Jerry indignantly.

The stripper stood up and raised his fists. He was a foot taller than Jerry and his greased muscles gleamed under the flashing backlights overhead.

"..Ah heh heh heh....I mean if you want to," Jerry apologized quickly, taking a step backward.

The stripper bounded forward, swung his fist backward and punched Jerry hard in the mouth. The blow knocked Jerry off of his feet and he slid across the dance floor, landing face-up several feet away. He sat up and spat a mouth full of blood and teeth onto the floor — and, while he was sitting there, wheezing and clutching his broken mouth, the stripper ran back toward him, with his fists raised. Ready to strike again.

Conrad stood up and put himself between Jerry and the stripper.

"*Hey*, he said, *get lost*, you stupid whore,"

Conrad boomed in the stripper's direction.

"Hey, fuck you, Conrad. Don't tell me this little piece of shit is your friend."

Conrad advanced on the stripper threateningly and the stripper retreated to avoid falling under Conrad's massive shadow.

"Ok, ok, man. Whatever. I'm gone," the stripper panicked, and then, he sprinted away and disappeared into the crowd.

Jerry stood and wiped the blood off of his face with the back of his hand. His expression grim, business like.

"Are you ok?" Conrad asked him.

"Fine," said Jerry impatiently. He removed a folded and crumpled piece of paper from his pocket and walked slowly forward with cold, calculated deliberation. For a moment, he staggered as though he were struggling to remain upright.

"Higgenmier was friends with the bouncer," Jerry informed Conrad very seriously. "Before he disappeared, he gave him — *this*"

Jerry unfolded the piece of paper and smoothed it flat. Printed on it was a glossy photograph of a naked woman who lay face up on a bed, staring into a camera that must have been positioned directly above her. She had long, wavy, sunflower yellow hair and looked very much like the woman from the photograph in Weston's slide show.

"It's the shman," Conrad remarked with amazement.

"Well it's *a* shman," said Jerry. "Probably not *the* shman we're looking for. If we were to bring this back to the lab and age date it, it might be over 200 years old."

"It looks so much like the shman we're looking for though," said Conrad. "What if it is him? What if this is a page from a recent magazine. It could mean that the rebels are protecting the shman to photograph it for profit."

"For profit? Who would pay for this?" Jerry interjected skeptically, brandishing the piece of paper in Conrad's face.

"I don't know," said Conrad taking the piece of paper out of Jerry's outstretched hand. "I might shell out some cash for this. He's hot.

Don't you think?"

"If by hot you mean completely fucking disgusting," Jerry said, "But I see your point. It's not impossible that this is a recent photograph. But it is unlikely. I still say we should bring it back to the lab and find out how old it is."

"Ok. That's fair," Conrad conceded. A part of him really didn't want to destroy the picture by carbon dating it. He liked the strange naked creature. It made him feel things when he looked at it.

Conrad flipped the magazine page over to see what there was on the back but the text there was too worn and damaged to read.

"What's this?" Conrad asked, pointing to the faded, illegible text on the other side of the page.

"I don't know," said Jerry. "But maybe the lab techs will have an answer for us. Are we done here?"

"Not yet," said Conrad. He lifted a key with a piece of tape on it. The number 22 was scribbled on the tape in black magic marker. "I got this from that stripper while he was giving me a lap dance."

"Where was he hiding it?" inquired Jerry.

Conrad laughed.

"He had it on a string around his neck. It was a bastard to untie without him noticing, but anyway, His name is Roy Harris and he just started working here. He said that the guy he replaced was 'this weird guy that disappeared

---

one day' and that he inherited his locker," said Conrad.

"But if there was anything left in that locker, don't you think that Roy would have already thrown it out?" said Jerry.

"Maybe," said Conrad. "But maybe not. He really didn't want to show me that locker. Which means that he's probably hiding something."

"What if that's not his locker key?" asked Jerry. He kept his voice even but staggered slightly, and then, ended his sentence by spitting more blood onto the floor.

"No. It is. The keys all look like this with the tape and the manager's ugly handwriting. Trust me. I used to work here," said Conrad and he pointed toward the back of the club with his thumb. "Come on, the lockers are this way."

Jerry began walking in the direction that Conrad was pointing and Conrad walked next to him. He extended a hand to steady Jerry's shoulder when he staggered again.

"You sure you ok?" said Conrad.

Jerry jerked away from Conrad as though the larger man's hand had burned him.

"Fine," he said. "Don't touch me."

Conrad reached a door at the back of the club. He inserted Roy's key into the key hole in the door knob, then, turned it. It clicked open.

"What exactly did Weston tell you about me before he assigned me as your partner?" said Conrad as he walked into the back room. Jerry followed. Conrad began searching the rows of lockers for the one that matched the number on Roy's key.

"Why? Did he tell you something about me?" Jerry asked.

"Mn...*nah*. What did he say?" Conrad asked again.

"Just one thing," said Jerry.

"Oh yea and what's that?" said Conrad, finding the locker marked twenty-two and sticking Roy's key into it.

"That you're the best," said Jerry.

"And do you know why he said that?" said Conrad, turning Roy's key so that the locker clicked unlocked.

"Why?"

Conrad opened the locker and grinned big at what he saw inside

"Because I'm the best, *buddy*," he finished pointing to the locker's contents with his thumb.

Jerry walked over to the locker and peered inside. It was papered with pictures of women both clothed and naked. Many looked as though they had been ripped out of magazines, both pornographic and non-pornographic. The sprawled, naked women were mixed in with old ladies in health insurance and diabetes adds, little girls holding hands with their mothers, and rotund pregnant women cradling infants. At the center of it was a diagram of a uterus with an unborn fetus in it. But neither Conrad nor Jerry knew what a uterus was and so neither Company Man was quite sure just what he was looking at.

"What on Earth...," Conrad murmured.

Spray painted over it all were the words "For Strange Lands Lucy."

"What's a Strange Lands Lucky?" Conrad murmured.

"I think it's a name," said Jerry quietly.

Jerry stared at the bizarre mural for a few moments longer than Conrad. And remained standing in front of the locker for minutes after Conrad walked away. *For Strange Lands Lucy*, the words were written there in large, purple, dripping letters, surrounded by photographs of what Jerry had been told for years were mythical creatures. Mythical creatures that aught not to have existed in photographs. Those words, *For Strange Lands Lucy*, sounded defiant when he read them in his head, they were a challenge to the government and The Company that had worked to erase Lucy from history. But what was more they were—

It was in that moment that Jerry, who prided himself on his stoicism and had not cried (even in private) for what must have been ten years, shed a single tear. Because in that moment he realized just what he was looking at. Not the work of a pervert delighting in an act of defiant exhibitionism, but rather, a sincere testament to a love most hazardous and illegal. A love that by Jerry's hands would end in blood and tragedy.

This was a shrine to a forbidden lover.

5

While Jerry had been taking in the illegal protest art, Conrad had tracked Roy Harris down in the strip club, tackled him, cuffed him and dragged him back to the convertible. Conrad grinned and waved at Jerry as he emerged from the strip club, then pointed to the suspect, Roy Harris, who was gagged and bound in the backseat. Jerry nodded grimly and got into the passenger seat.

"Wow," Jerry said, fastening his seatbelt, and then, adjusting his glasses by pushing them up in the center with his index finger. "You really are the best."

"You know it," said Conrad and he revved

the engine of the convertible, speeding off into the distance.

"For a minute there you had me fooled," said Jerry.

Roy shrieked some profanities that were muffled by his gag. Conrad took a sharp turn, causing Roy to topple sideways and smash his head against the side of the car.

"Yea, you thought I was a buffoon, did ya'?" said Conrad.

"Honestly, yes."

"Sometimes it's good to make people think that," said Conrad, speeding through a red light. A barrage of screeching car horns, breaks and pissed-off drivers assaulted Jerry's ears, and then, Conrad screamed "Oh yea, well fuck you and *both* yo' Daddy's!" out the window in retaliation. The car swerved while he was doing this and Jerry reached out to steady the wheel with one shaking hand. While Jerry was doing this, the case folders, which had been resting in his lap, flew out of the window.

"Son of a fucking bastard!" Jerry swore as he watched his folders fly away and into the distance.

"That's why you should use a stick drive, grandpa," said Conrad jovially.

"That was classified information, *Conrad*," grumbled Jerry.

Conrad laughed a long, hard, and deep laugh. He pointed to the folders being carried into the distance, and then, to Jerry's face, reddening with anger, and then, closed his eyes and clutched his side with his free hand. Leaving the wheel completely untouched once again.

"Stop it. Stop laughing. It's not funny," said Jerry. "I take what I said back. You drive like a fucking idiot."

Conrad put his hands back on the wheel and turned his face back toward the road.

"You think I'm a moron, huh?" Conrad asked with in a slightly aggressive tone, flashing Jerry a dangerous, intimidating glower.

"I think you're a fucking idiot," Jerry confirmed with a cold and indifferent bluntness.

"Heh. Most people crap their pants when I ask them that question," Conrad remarked, grinning jovially. He pulled into a parking space in front of the ice-cube-shaped building that was The Company and then added. "I like you Jerry, you've got this whole frumpy doofus thing goin' on that I really dig."

"Uh huh," Jerry replied skeptically. He wasn't sure whether he should take this as an insult or a complement.

"And if I keep my mouth shut about you loosing those folders, I hope that you'll reconsider the sex with me," said Conrad.

"Tell anyone you want about the folders," said Jerry angrily, pointing accusingly in Conrad's direction. "You don't touch me. Ever. Got that."

Conrad laughed again.

"Your loss. My dick's like eight feet long," he bragged.

"Don't care." said Jerry crossly.

"Relax. I was only kidding."

"Were you?"

Conrad got out of the car and pulled Roy out of the back seat.

"Cooperate with The Company. If you resist, I am authorized to terminate your life," Conrad said to Roy as he walked him into the building. This was a set phrase that Company Men were supposed to recite to criminal suspects upon capture.

Roy grumbled something that was muffled by the gag but did not resist. It was common knowledge that Company Men were authorized to terminate the life of a suspect that resisted capture, and Roy, like many of the residents of Mantropolis had witnessed this fact first hand. Once when he was seven and once when he was seventeen. He remembered it now. Two bullets were fired, to the side of two heads, point blank. Two squirting, headless corpses crumbled to the floor and slid down two blood splattered walls. Both versions of his former self watched with open-mouthed horror.

And so, Roy walked with Conrad into The Company building without a struggle.

6

Danny Churchill was The Company torture guy. His office was a little rectangular, mostly empty room, with white walls, a plain white desk, and a spinning computer chair. The wall behind his chair was made of one-way glass and looked out into the interrogation room. The interrogation room was simply a large, empty room, painted white and illuminated by rows of fluorescent lights in the ceiling.

Conrad and Jerry entered Churchill 's office and stood in front of his desk.

"Hello," Churchill greeted them broadly. He was very skinny with sunken cheeks, mocha-colored skin, and dark, curly, greased-up hair that he had tied up in a disheveled pony tail. He wore a black, high-collared jacket embroidered with the insignia of The Company over black slacks and a black polo shirt. His shoes were shiny and black and his socks were black. Pretty much everything that Churchill owned, excluding this room, was black, as Conrad (who had worked with Churchill for years) could attest. Rumor had it that, Churchill enjoyed his job a bit more than he let on. But Conrad (who had worked with Churchill for years) could not decipher with any degree of accuracy whether or not this was true. The man was a quiet, efficient enigma.

Jerry, who had done office work for The Company until this point, and had never met Churchill before, greeted him nervously. Conrad, who was never really uncomfortable around anybody, greeted Churchill like an old friend.

"Danny!" he shouted reaching over the

desk to shake Churchill 's hand. "How are you? How have you been?"

"Excellent," Churchill replied seriously. "Shall we begin?"

"Please," replied Jerry, picturing that lonely plate of leftover spaghetti in his refrigerator at home, waiting to be eaten. "Let's get this over with."

"Very well then," said Churchill. He pulled a black plastic remote control out of his pocket and flipped one of the metal switches on it. The lights in the interrogation room flickered on behind him. Roy appeared in one of the corners of the interrogation room, alone and unbound. He was curled into a ball with his arms wrapped around his calves to shield his mostly naked body from the cold.

"He can't see us through this one way glass," said Churchill to Jerry incase he was unaware of how this worked. "But he can hear us."

Churchill pushed another button on his remote and spoke into a microphone on his desk.

"Who is Strange Lands Lucy?" he asked quietly.

"Strange Lands Lucy is nobody! She's not real, man! She's just a legend!" Roy shouted back in a panic.

Churchill pushed another button on his remote and a massive scorpion-like creature with a number of massive purple eyes dropped from the ceiling in the interrogation room. Roy stood up quickly and sprinted away from it. The thing chased him and he ran around the room in circles to stop the thing from striking him with its crab-like pincers, and scorpion-like flailing needle tail.

"No one can keep their lies straight when they're running for their life," Churchill explained for Jerry's benefit.

"Who is Strange Lands Lucy!" Conrad shouted into the microphone on Churchill's desk.

"She's just a legend, man! A story! She's not even a real person!" Roy shouted as he was running from the monster.

"Why did you have those pictures in your

locker?" Churchill asked.

"They weren't mine, man! They were Higgenmeir's! I tried to tell your...," Roy paused to gasp for breath and glance behind him as the creature advanced. Then, began running again. "...Your fuckin' stooge before he gagged me, man! Higgenmier super glued those pictures to the inside of his locker probably the night before he left. When I got the job at the strip club and I found the pictures in my locker, I...I knew I'd get in trouble for having them, so I didn't tell anyone they were there! I.....I tried to to....to tear them off but they were stuck real....really....good. But I was gonna' paint over them, man! I swear to god, man! You have to believe me."

"I don't *have* to do anything," Churchill

replied coldly.   "Why did you have those pictures in your locker?"

Roy replied between gasps of air, with what was more or less the same story. Churchill asked him a third time and Roy replied a third time with what was more or less the same story.

Churchill pushed a button on his remote to mute the speaker.

"I believe him," Churchill said.

Churchill pushed the button on his remote again to un-mute the speaker.

"What do you know about Strange Lands Lucy?" Churchill asked.

"Nothing," said Roy.   "Because she's not fucking real, you psycho! She's just a story!"

"Tell me about the story, then."

Roy stopped running for a moment to catch his breath. The monster slowed to a stop and stared at him with its one massive, purple eye. Its single pupil dilated and its fanged mouth fell open, drooling.

"Get...get rid of that thing," Roy gasped.

"Very well," complied Churchill. He pushed a button on his remote and the monster fell through a trap door in the floor of the interrogation room. "Tell the story."

"They say.... that twenty years ago, the birthing factory accidentally switched a male with a shmale infant....they say that the male infant had its limbs and head circumcised to grow as an incubator and....and the shmale infant was given to a couple to raise. As she grew she became more and more savage until she was too hard for them to raise, so they brought her out to the Strange Lands and released her in the desert....and she kills people and rips their hearts out and uses their blood as an exfoliate mask. It's really fucking stupid. Have you heard enough yet?"

"Tell the rest of the story," commanded Churchill .

"Ok, ok, fine," said Roy quickly, and then, he continued his story. "They say that Strange Lands Lucy is the daughter of the Devil himself and the mother of the one who will destroy us all. Her voice is so shrill and unpleasant that it shatters glass and makes whoever hears it permanently deaf. And instead of a penis, there's a gross hole between her legs that she uses to squirt blood at people, like a squid. If it gets in your eyes, it'll make you go blind or see demons or something like that. Or maybe you'll stink forever and then turn into a zombie. It really depends on who you ask. If she sees a man lost in the desert, she starts screaming and shitting herself while she jumps up and down and it makes her gross chest flaps flop around, so that the man becomes a hypnotized, vicious, drooling beast. Then, I think he also shits himself. And then I think, according to some people, Lucy can fly, but then according to some people, she just shits herself so hard that she shoots up into the air....or something."

"Yes, yes, I get it. Everyone is shitting

themselves. Let's move on please," interjected Churchill .

"They say that if you say her name three times in the mirror after midnight, she'll jump out from behind the glass and bite your penis off. And that on her twenty-first birthday, on the night of the red moon, she will choose a lover who will be the new king of this world and the father of the beast who will slay The Overlords. I think it was that part that Higgenmier used to like. I met him once for about ten minutes, right after he left the strip club and right before he disappeared and he talked a lot about that part. He said that he wanted Lucy to be his lover and that he wanted to be the ruler of the new world."

"Who told you this story, Roy?" Churchill asked.

"I don't know. It's just a story," said Roy. "It's something people talk about. Don't you listen to people?"

"I only listen to smooth jazz," said Churchill .

"Where did this rumor start?" Jerry asked.

"Jesus, Joseph, and Manny! I don't know!" Roy swore.

"Hm. Must be a Catholic," Conrad mumbled.

"Just let me go, man! I swear to God, I told you everything I know!"

Churchill shrugged.

"I don't believe him," he said and then he

pushed a button on his remote, releasing a second purple scorpion beast into the interrogation room. This time the thing landed on top Roy him, pinning him underneath of its massive body. Roy shrieked and thrashed wildly in an attempt to free himself but it was of no use. He was trapped.

"Tell me what you know fast or I'll let it kill you," said Churchill evenly.

"It's going to kill him, Churchill," said Jerry. "How can you even stop it?"

"I'm glad you asked, Jerry," said Churchill. "The interrogation room is equip with a ventilation system which can filter in a neurotoxin call zefferpeberin polly-pseudo-bicarbonate or zeppbic, if you prefer. It's a chemical, which is only deadly to Strange Lands Beasts."

"Ok. Interesting. Shouldn't you be stopping it from killing him now?" said Jerry.

For the first time since Jerry and Conrad had entered his office, Churchill spun his chair around and faced the interrogation room. The Strange Lands scorpion beast lowered its massive head slowly, and its cross-shaped lips peeled themselves backwards to reveal four rows of dripping, razor sharp fangs.

"What else do you know?" Churchill asked quietly.

"I- I told you I don't know anything!"

"Don't move," Churchill advised him. "If you move it'll kill you faster."

Roy began praying.

"...H-hail Manny, other father of God...," he sputtered.

"You know something," said Churchill calmly. "What is it?"

"...B-blessed art thou a among men and blessed is the fru-fruit of thou surrogate incubator spawn, Jesus," Roy prayed.

"Stop praying and tell us. What do you know Roy?" Churchill said.

"H-holy Manny, other f-father of God. Pray for us sinners. Now and at the hour of our d-d-de-death   aaAAAAGHHHHHHH! AAAaaaGGGGGHHHHHH! AAAAAAAAAAAGGGGGGGHHHHHHHHHH!"

Roy shrieked as the monster bit down on the top of his head and popped it off like the top of an Easter egg. He kicked the monster wildly and beat it with his fists but the monster was not damaged by his blows. It only became enraged and let out a shrill, rattling *ka cahw* as it chomped off the rest of his head.

"Oops," said Churchill indifferently. "Looks like I killed him."

7

"Shit. Oh shit. Fatherfucker that was dark!" Jerry swore and then he bit his lower lip so hard that a trickle of blood spilled out from under his broken teeth.

"Yea, killing is part of the job," said Conrad calmly. "It took me a little while to get used to it too."

The two men exited the company building and walked out into the parking lot.

"Well, I miss desk work," said Jerry hoarsely. Now when he went home and ate his left over pasta he would be thinking about a dead stripper's stringy shredded brains drenched in blood the whole time, and not enjoy it.

"Well," said Conrad, checking his watch. "The shift's over. See you tomorrow, Jerry."

"Nope. No you won't," said Jerry indignantly. "Because, I am getting myself transferred back to the clerical department. " *I* am a *criminal profile sketch man*......not a *murder man*!"

"Aw, but I was just starting to like you," said Conrad.

"Do you always flirt with people before you kill them?" Jerry growled, his magnified eyes locking onto Conrad's small blue ones.

For once Conrad was at a loss for words, very surprised by the smaller man's bold comment.

"I...uh...," Conrad stumbled.

"And your friend, Churchill . Nope. Uhuh. No. Keep 'im far away from me," said Jerry shaking his head.

"Oh him, yea...he's just a crazy guy. Totally cool. I swear. You'll get used to him," said Conrad.

"Good bye, Conrad," Jerry said.

"Hopefully forever." And then he stalked away.

"Uh. Bye," murmured Conrad. He walked over to his red convertible and jumped in the driver's side seat, then, peeled out of the parking space and sped away.

That night, Conrad dreamed about Strange Lands Lucy. She stood at the center of a wide, cobble stone bridge, over a lake in Mantropolis City Park, still and quiet. It was raining and she was holding a pink umbrella trimmed in white lace. Conrad ran towards her but she turned and walked away. She was moving slowly but he couldn't catch her. He saw only the back of her sunflower yellow head, the long, pink, frilly shirt from Weston's photograph, and pink rubber boots, sloshing slowly through growing puddles.

"Lucy, wait! Come back!" Conrad called after her.

Lucy turned toward him slowly and her sunflower yellow hair spun around her like a gorgeous blond tornado. She was silent and watched him with large blue eyes and pert painted lips.

"I want to...I want to stick my penis in your crotch hole!" Conrad blurted out before she could turn around and start walking away again.

Lucy's smooth face shriveled and melted into that of a pock-marked, vomit green beast, then, she opened her cross-shaped mouth wide, revealing four pairs of razor sharp fangs. She screamed like Roy while he was getting his head ripped off, spitting blood in Conrad's face. The sky turned red. The rain became blood and stringy chunks of shredded brains.

Conrad woke. He jumped out of bed and lifted his mattress, to see if the illegal naked picture of Lucy that he had snuck back with him, was still there. It was. He put the mattress back down over it, and stumbled over to his refrigerator to retrieve a couple of beers.

8

The next day, Conrad saw Jerry in The Company lobby.

"Jerry, Hey!" he called, waving at him and grinning big. Jerry nodded grimly in response. "Did you get your desk job back?"

"Uh. No, actually. The human resources director is refusing to take my calls," said Jerry.

"Alright, then. Let's roll," said Conrad, gesturing toward the exit of the building with both thumbs.

Jerry lagged behind him, watching him coldly as he exited the building and disappeared into the parking lot.

"You know, it's driving him crazy that you don't like him," Churchill said, emerging from behind a tall decorative plant in the lobby. Jerry, startled by Churchill's sudden appearance, jumped backward, shielding his face with his hands. Then, quickly regained his reserved demeanor, smoothing his shirt and adjusting the bridge of his glasses with his index finger.

"He acts like it's not. But it is. Conrad wants *everyone* to like him." Churchill said and somehow his quiet slow voice was even creepier in the relative normalcy of the lobby than it had been in the interrogation room.

"Um..."

"No matter *how* insignificant they are. It's really a rather exploitable eccentricity," he finished darkly.

"Uh. Ok. Noted," said Jerry uncomfortably, and then, he sprinted away from Churchill and toward the door.

<u>2</u>

Jerry climbed into the passenger seat of Conrad's car and put his seatbelt on, his expression stern, wooden. He glanced at

Conrad cautiously and Conrad grinned back, opened a beer and took a long, slow, drag from it.

"You want one?" he asked Jerry, putting his half-finished beer down in the cup holder between them.

"I'll pass," Jerry replied disgustedly.

Conrad shrugged.

"Eh. Suit yourself.

He started the car and peeled out of the parking lot, shooting out onto the highway. Jerry grimaced, every time Conrad ignored a stop sign or rolled through a red light, but resisted the urge to say something about it. He had the feeling that Conrad would have taken criticism about his driving as a challenge to drive even faster.

"Uh...Arnold Copperfield's father's apartment is that way," said Jerry as Conrad sped past the exit they were supposed to have been taking. He pointed backward at the exit even though Conrad wasn't really looking at him or paying attention to what he was saying.

"Don't care," Conrad said. "This way is faster."

"...*Is it* faster?"

"Yea, sure it is. Probably. We're making really good time," said Conrad.

The two men were silent for awhile.

"Copperfield's father still lives in the apartment. I contacted him on the phone last night and he agreed to meet with us between the hours of 8:00 a.m. and 11:00 a.m. about his missing son," said Jerry, hoping to impress upon Conrad how important it was that they honor this appointment.

"We don't need him to agree to anything. We're Company Men. He has to talk to us when we tell him to. And if he doesn't we just," Conrad slid this thumb across his throat and made a low choking noise, "kill him."

"We're not going to *kill* him, Conrad," said Jerry a little indignantly.

"I doubt we'll have to."

"He's lost his son, in a way," Jerry argued. "He'll be grieving, I imagine, and I'm sure he'll be much more cooperative if we come at a time that's convenient for him."

"Ok. Whatever. If it makes you feel better, I'll make sure we get there by ei—oh my holy crap, it's the double quadruple bacon man burger!" Conrad shouted, pointing at a large sign with a picture of a gigantic, eight-patty-thick cheeseburger with a thick layer of bacon sandwiched between each thick, greasy slab of meat. The impossible to eat sandwich was laying sensuously on a white plate with a side of deep-fried bacon and two tubs of barbeque dipping sauce. Above this picture, were printed the words: "Double Quadruple Bacon Man Burger!!! For a limited time!!! Only at Lardo's Lard Shack!!! Eat one or you're a pussy!!!"

"The double quadruple bacon man burger, Jerry!" Conrad shouted ecstatically, grabbing the collar of Jerry's blue suit jacket with both hands and shaking him. "Its only here for a limited time!"

Conrad veered off the road and into the Lardo's Lard Shack parking lot.

"Conrad, this is off task!" Jerry shouted quickly as Conrad parked and jumped over the diver's side door of his car, bolting toward the entrance of the restaurant.

A few minutes passed and Conrad re-emerged holding two, large, greasy fast food bags.

He jumped back in the car and started driving again, holding the wheel with one hand and the massive burger with the other. The car swerved and a man in a large, blue truck blew his horn and swore at Conrad. Conrad took his other hand off of the wheel to flash the guy his middle finger while he screamed "Fuck you!" Jerry grabbed the wheel to stop the car from swerving again.

"You know, maybe you shouldn't try to eat that while you're driving?" Jerry suggested cautiously.

"You don't have to be jealous. I got one for you too," said Conrad, pointing to a second greasy bag on the floor of the car.

"Heh...thanks, but I'm a vegetarian," said Jerry.

"What you don't each double quadruple bacon man burgers?"

"Really   nothing   from   fast   food

restaurants," said Jerry.

"What are you a masochist? Eat the sandwich."

"Conrad. I told you. I'm a vegetarian. Just drive and leave me alone, ok?" said Jerry.

"C'mon, bro, I'm trying to do something nice for you. Eat the sandwich. You're too skinny," insisted Conrad.

"I'm not eating the sandwich, Conrad."

"Eat the sandwich or you're a pussy."

"I don't even know what that is," said Jerry exasperatedly.

"It's a cat. You know like....meow meow...I'm a cat....meow meow....I only eat saucers of milk and crap that comes out of a can...because I'm a cat," Conrad mocked .

"Ehhehehheh...cats are stupid."

"This shit you're doing with the stupid cat voice," said Jerry. "It's off task. Let's stick to the case, ok?"

"Whatever, pussy, why don't you run off and chase mice or something? Take a nap. Run after a plastic bag blowing down the street," Conrad teased, grinning. "Because you're a cat."

"God damn it, *I hate cats!*" Jerry shouted. "If I eat the stupid bread, will you shut up?"

"Maybe if you don't get too distracted by a piece of string first," Conrad mocked.

Jerry opened the fast food bag, took the two greasy, sauce-soaked buns off of the sandwich, and shoved them both into his mouth.

"There, see that, Conrad, I'm eating the

bread. The bread is in my mouth. I'm eating the bread," gargled Jerry spastically through a mouth full of hamburger bun. "Are you happy, now?"

"Yes."

"Then, shut up."

After about an hour of driving, Jerry and Conrad reached the apartment complex where Arnold Copperfield's father lived. It was a tall, brick building with a white door. Conrad pulled over, parked the car, jumped over the driver's side door, and walked toward the building. Jerry opened the passenger's side door, stepped out onto the blacktop, and followed him reluctantly. He shuffled his feet as he walked, put his hands in his pockets, and assumed a serious, business-like expression.

The two men entered the building, walked past the door man in the lobby and straight toward the door with the room 102 printed on it. Jerry extended a bony knuckle and thumped the door a few times. He lowered his hand and waited. There was silence for a few moments. Then, the door creaked open. An old man with a grey mustache and a bald head like the broad side of an egg, peered out at them through a crack in the door. A short copper chain in the wall was pulled taunt, and stopped the door from opening any further.

"What do you want?" the old man asked morosely. His blue eyes narrowed beneath the square lenses of his wire-framed glasses.

"Are you Arnold Copperfield Sr.?" Jerry inquired politely.

"I am," said the old man.

"We're Company Men, here to ask you a few questions about your son," said Jerry and he flashed his Company I.D. at Copperfield. Conrad, who was standing behind Jerry, did the same.

Copperfield unhooked the bronze chain from the door and let it swing open the rest of the way.

"Come in," he said, sounding very unenthusiastic.

Copperfield walked past an umbrella stand filled with different colored umbrellas, and decorative wooden walking sticks, into the living room, which contained a tan leather sofa and loveseat, a wooden coffee table and a large flat screen television. The walls were painted tan and the kitchen was visible through a gap in the dark-stained cabinets.

"I wish you had gotten here before eleven," droned Copperfield miserably. "I have to go to work."

"I apologize for the delay, Mr. Copperfield," said Jerry, "But I assure you that my partner and I got here as quickly as was possible."

"Yea, well its 11. So...I'm going to work now," said Copperfield, rolling his eyes.

"No. You're not," barked Conrad. The sound of his unusually deep voice made

Copperfield flinch. "Sit down. We have a few questions to ask you about your missing son."

"You didn't find him, did you?" inquired Copperfield skeptically.

"No. That's not what this is about," said Conrad.

Copperfield sat down on the leather sofa. Conrad sat down next to him and Jerry sat down on the horizontally adjacent loveseat.

"We're truly sorry for your loss, Mr. Copperfield," said Jerry. "But we do believe that your son is alive. With a properly conducted investigation..."

"Spare me the crap, agent," Copperfield interrupted rather caustically. "I know as well as anybody what becomes of those Lucy freaks."

"So your son was a follower of Lucy?" Jerry inquired.

"Is that what they're calling it?" Copperfield said, sounding disgusted. "I swear, agent. I tried to teach that boy right from wrong. Lord knows I tried. The kid was never right. He struggled with some..."

The room got quiet for a moment and Jerry and Conrad stared at Copperfield, waiting for him to finish his sentence.

"*Latent heterosexual tendencies...*" Copperfield finished reluctantly.

"What did your son tell you about Lucy?" Jerry asked.

"You're asking me what my son told me about a fictional creature?" Copperfield scoffed.

"What are you investigating next? The unicorn and leprechaun wars?"

"Answer the question," Conrad growled. "Why we want to know is none of your damn business."

"He said all kinds of really disgusting things...Jesus forgive me for repeating them," said Copperfield. "He said that Lucy was a creature called a woman....and that she was like a man but instead of a penis she has something called a....a....*vamrina*."

"What's a vamrina?" Conrad asked.

"He said it was like a gross sticky hole or something like that," said Copperfield. "It's fucking stupid, but anyway. My kid tells me he wants to stick his penis in a vamrina. So I tell him, kid, you don't even think about sticking your penis in a shman's vamrina!"

"Right," said Jerry, nodding soberly. "Go on."

"And then I tell him the truth, that there are no living shmen. Shmen, are deformed stillborn children, son, this story about how they can get older and learn how to talk is just liberal nonsense, I say. And he says, no Dad, shmen are real! I swear they are! There's one named Lucy and she's alive. She can talk and walk around on her own and everything! The naive little ungrateful idiot, is sinning against God, like I didn't teach him common decency! It's *Addam and Steve* not Addam and *Eve*! Vamrina's aren't even a real thing, they're just grotesque deformities on non-viable fetuses, and he's plenty old enough to know that! These stories are how Satanists recruit their followers, and turn people against the teaching of Jesus Christ, and against wholesome family values that I tried to teach my son. God knows I tried to teach him to respect God's laws. God knows. I just hope he comes to his senses soon, so he doesn't wind up in hell with those other freaks," said Copperfield.

"When was the last time you saw your son, Mr. Copperfield?" Jerry asked.

"About six months ago," said Copperfield. "He had just met this really nice guy, classically handsome, with really wavy black hair, such a nice guy...and I thought, finally, my son's ready to settle down, you know, marry a nice boy and put all of this childish shmen stuff behind him? Finally Glen can stop rolling in his grave."

"Glen?" Jerry inquired.

"My late husband. He died when Arnold was little."

"So, this guy, he was your son's boyfriend?" Conrad asked.

"That's what I thought," said Copperfield. "But then I find out that they're not even dating! Instead they're both talking about shmen all the time like they're a real thing. They have these naked pictures of men, Photoshopped to look like shmen, and they're talking about them like they're real....And then this guy, this beautiful, handsome guy that my son won't sleep with, who can have any man in the world that he wants, he tells me that he's a...*a*...."

The room got quiet for a moment and Jerry and Conrad both stared at Copperfield, waiting for him to finish his sentence.

"A...*heterosexual*," Copperfield whispered reluctantly, as though the word itself might contaminate him.

"What was this man's name?" Conrad asked.

"Dick Johnson," said Copperfield.

"And he met your son—"

"At the construction sight, right," Copperfield confirmed.

"He was a construction worker?" Conrad asked.

"Yes."

"And where was the construction site where your son and Mr. Johnson met?" Jerry asked.

"They were building a new wing onto the birthing factory," said Copperfield. "You should have heard the naive little idiot. The factory opened my eyes, Dad! Pops saw it too before he died! Lucy is *real*! Jesus forgive him....my son makes up stories to get attention. I don't know where I went wrong."

"Your son lived with you for awhile, right?" Conrad asked.

"Right," Copperfield confirmed.

"Is his stuff still in the house?" Conrad asked.

"Some of it. After he disappeared, I threw a lot of it out," said Copperfield. He had, in fact, meticulously burned any illegal record of the existence of shmen that his son had left in his room before his disappearance.

"Which room was it?" Conrad asked.

Copperfield pointed to a wooden door off the side of the living room.

"Go through that door and down the hall. It's the third door on your left," said Copperfield.

Conrad stood up.

"C'mon, Jerry let's go," he said, motioning toward the door that Copperfield had indicated."

Jerry stood up and followed Conrad toward the door. Copperfield Sr. stood up as well, a look of concern, twisting his lined face.

"Please, if you do find my son. Promise me that you won't kill him straight away. He's a good boy. He'll snap out of this thing one of these days. Just promise me you'll put him in a mental institution, not a morgue."

"I promise," said Jerry, turning his head to look Copperfield in the eyes. They were glossy with unshed tears, and caught the light of the decorative lamp overhead, giving them the appearance of shiny blue-centered marbles. There was some genuine affection for his son there, surely, despite their differences.

"I promise nothing," grunted Conrad indifferently.

<u>10</u>

Arnold Copperfield's room was almost completely empty. Conrad and Jerry searched the room thoroughly and found nothing but a bare mattress on a plain, square, black bed frame, a wooden desk, with empty drawers, a swiveling computer chair, and an old grey computer. The computer was a thick, heavy laptop with sticky keys that smelled like day-old pizza and dirty socks. The walls around it were white and littered with pieces of clear tape.

"Jeeze, do you think Arnold whacked himself off while holding this computer?" Jerry shuttered, having noticed the suspicious stickiness of the keys, when he pushed them to see if the screen on the computer would light up.

"Yea, probably. Who wouldn't, right?" said Conrad. "Is it coming on?"

Jerry stared at the screen for a moment and tapped a few of the keys at random. This made the monitor light up. A black screen with an empty text box under the word: password appeared. Jerry typed the word "Lucy" into the box and pressed enter. Nothing happened. He tried again but this time typed "lucy" with a lower case L. Still, nothing happened.

"Try vagrima," grunted Conrad. He found a leftover piece of deep fried bacon in the pocket of his pants and popped it in his mouth, crunching loudly.

Jerry typed the word "vagina" into the computer. The black screen disappeared and now he was looking at an open email.

"How did you *know* that?" Jerry asked, sounding both incredulous and impressed.

Conrad Shrugged.

"I dunno."

"Conrad, look at this," said Jerry very seriously.

"Is it more porn?" Conrad inquired hopefully.

"No," said Jerry.

"Aw. Damn it."

"This is an email correspondence between Arnold Copperfield and someone claiming to be Strange Lands Lucy," said Jerry.

Conrad glanced at the screen and read the open email:

Ms. Lucy: I can't wait to meet you, vaginalover666! I get so lonely out here in The Sands with no one for company but Killer! He's my dog. He's an Irish Wolf Hound. I know you'll love him. He's so cute! Here's a picture of me and Killer!

Underneath of this message was an attachment.

"Click on the attachment," Conrad said. Perhaps Lucy was naked in the picture. Conrad hoped that Lucy was naked in the picture.

Jerry clicked on the attachment. A blurry picture of a shman with wavy blond hair, smiling big and hugging a massive Irish Wolf Hound to her ample chest appeared. Conrad was disappointed to see that Lucy was dressed. She wore a bright pink shirt and a pair of loose-fitting jeans. There were pink dogwood flowers braided into her hair and yellow sand all around her. The desert seemed to stretch on and on into the distance.

Jerry scrolled down to read Arnold Copperfield's reply:

vaginalover666: Cute dog.   Wanna fuck? Where you at, bro?

Ms. Lucy: I'm in the Strange Lands!   Come and find me!!! ;) ;) ;)

vaginalover666: Where in the Strange Lands?

Ms. Lucy: I can't tell you : (: (: (The Manazonians will find out and kill me!

vinginalover666: Then, give me a clue.

Ms. Lucy: Okey dokey!!!

I am a clue. I am hiding at the beginning and

at the end. My number is 9999 and my home is the instrument of life and death. No one will see me. Because I am forbidden. No one will notice me. Because I am less interesting than the other things. Come find me.

"Do you have any idea what the hell all of that means, Jerry?" Conrad asked incredulously, scratching his head.

"No. But it doesn't matter. The guys in the computer lab can just trace the email and find out where it was sent from. It should lead us straight to her," said Jerry. Then, he snapped the lap top shut, unplugged it from the wall, and rolled up its chord.

"Arnold must have known what it meant...because he found Lucy," Conrad mused.

"Yea, he must have," agreed Jerry.

That night, Conrad dreamed about Lucy again. She was standing on the bridge over the lake in Mantropolis Central Park. It was raining and she was carrying a lacy pink camisole, twirling it in her hands as she skipped through growing puddles. Her pink rain boots made rhythmic sloshing sounds as they kicked through clear, cold water. Conrad couldn't see her face. He could only see the back of her sunflower yellow head and the twirling camisole. Her long, lacy, pink shirt rippled in a nonexistent breeze.

"Lucy! Wait!" Conrad called, running after her. His legs were heavy like bricks. It took all of his energy to keep them moving.

"Wait for me!"

Lucy spun around, her sparkling sunflower locks, glistened with rain water, flying through the air like a golden tornado. Her painted lips stretched into a slow smile and her bright blue eyes grew wide. She stared at Conrad as though she were enamored with him.

"I'm so lonely here, Conrad!" she exclaimed perkily. Her voice was very high-pitched. "The Manazonians don't want to play with me! And that makes me *sad*!"

"Lucy...I.....*I*....," Conrad stuttered.

Just then, an Irish Wolf hound appeared out of no where, grabbed Conrad's balls in its mouth, and ripped them off. A torrent of blood squirted all over Lucy's demented, grinning face.

And she giggled creepily. Like a monster in a horror movie.

Conrad's eyes shot open and he sat bolt upright in his bed, Lucy's sadistic laugh still ringing in his ears.

<u>11</u>

Jerry held Arnold Copperfield's large, heavy computer with both hands. Its grey extension cord was coiled into a tight bungle and dangled off of the side of the machine. The cord swayed as he walked up several flights of winding, white steps to The Company computer department. He took his time both a) because he was not looking forward to his conversation with The Company computer guys (who where not very fond of Jerry and really saw him as a joke) and b) because the computer was so damn heavy that he was afraid that he might drop it. He gripped that ancient grey monstrosity with white, bloodless fingers. Sweat prickled his brow. He was beginning to feel the machine slip. And now his arms were starting to ache from carrying it. He reached the top of the steps, collapsed onto the ground, and rested briefly, wiping the sweat off of his forehead and adjusting his large glasses. Then, he took a deep breath straightened up, and walked through the door at the top of the steps into the computer department.

"Heey, *Jeeery!*" a man with large, thick glasses greeted him. The man was tinkering with a large, white computer, removing its plastic shell, and then, the tiny metal pieces underneath. The man, himself, was young, with neatly parted brown hair and a stubble beard.

"Laurence, hi," Jerry replied coldly.

"This is perfect! We were just talking about you," said Laurence, he turned to the man sitting next to him, who was young, pale, and had a lot of really curly blond hair that stood up on his head like an afro. "Tony, ask him how much he can bench press. Go ahead, ask him!"

Tony put down the screwdriver he was holding and looked up at Jerry, who was still standing there, struggling to hold onto Arnold Copperfeild's laptop. The table that the two computer guys were working on was covered in machine parts and there was really no place to put it down. Jerry was reluctant to put the computer down on the floor, however. The computer department guys surely would have found that amusing.

"How much can you bench press, Jerry?" Tony asked.

"That's not important. Right now I need you to look at this laptop for me. Could you clear a space so I can put it down?" Jerry said quickly.

"Why, you about to drop it?" Tony mocked disparagingly.

Both Tony and Laurence laughed.

"*No*. Will you take a look at the computer?"

"Hey, hey, hey not so fast, bro-padochip.

How much can you bench press?" asked Laurence again, grinning evilly.

"Two hundred pounds," Jerry lied, staring Laurence down.

This made Laurence and Tony bust out laughing.

"Oh God, oh Christ! Pah hah hah! Did you hear hear that, Tony!" Laurence laughed clutching his side. "Two-ha ha-ha-two hundred pounds!"

"Careful, he might beat us up!" Tony laughed.

"But seriously, how much can you really bench press?" Laurence asked.

"Like 40 pounds, is that what you want to hear? Just look at the computer, ok? The person who owned this computer had an email conversation with someone who might be a person marked for death by the—"

Laurence and Tony started laughing again. And now they were laughing so hard that Jerry couldn't hear himself talk.

"Jerry, *Jerry*, how many push-ups can you do?" Laurence asked.

"Fifty," lied Jerry. "Now this computer—"

Laurence and Tony started laughing again.

"We hacked into your records. How many push-ups can you *really* do?" Tony asked, grinning.

"I can do *one*," Jerry muttered with a groan. "Is that what you want to hear? Now this computer."

Laurence and Tony burst into another fit of hysterical laugher.

"Oh god, oh hahaha ha ha...oh fucking Jesus, that's pathetic!" Laurence cackled.

"Hahaha...Dude, my Grandpa can do more pushups than you and he's 87!"

"Ha ha. Good one. That's very amusing. Now, this computer—"

Jerry swept his arm across the table, and knocked a bunch of machine parts onto the floor, then, put the computer down in front of them. Laurence and Tony stared at him for a moment, finally silent.

"Not cool, bro," Tony said.

"There's an email on this computer," Jerry

said. He tapped a few keys on the computer and the screen lit up with the emailed conversation between Arnold Copperfield and Strange Lands Lucy. Jerry pointed to the screen. "Here it is. The person who calls himself Ms. Lucy? I want you to find out where he's sending these emails from. Can you do that for me?"

Laurence and Tony stared at Jerry for a moment with blank expressions. Then, they broke into another fit of uncontrollable laughter.

"Hahaha oh God, oh fucking Christ...HAHA ha ha!" Laurence guffawed, spinning around in his swivel chair.

"Phht!! Hahaaaha! Yea, we'll get hahAHAHA! We'll get on that *right away!*" Tony cackled sarcastically.

"Yea. Ok. Thanks," said Jerry coldly and he trudged out of the room, his expression stiff, impassive.

<u>12</u>

Days passed. Jerry visited The Company computer department every day and every day the guys working there told him that they had not gotten around to tracing the email yet. They had more important things to do. A whole list of them, apparently.

"Yea, we have a list of priorities," said Carl Sanders, an older man with grey hair and square, wire-framed glasses. He was the head of The Company Computer Department and much less rowdy than some of his younger co-workers.

"May I see the list?" Jerry asked coldly.

"No," said Sanders. "But I assure you there is one. It is very long. And it definitely exists."

"Why can't I see the list, then?" Jerry asked.

"No," said Sanders.

Jerry sighed.

"Can you get me an estimate on how much time it'll take for your crew to get around to the email, then?" Jerry asked.

Sanders lifted his coffee mug up to his cracked lips and slurped its contents slowly.

"Probably about.....uhhh......*4 weeks*?" said Sanders.

"4 weeks?" Jerry repeated incredulously.

"Is there anyway you could get to it sooner than that?"

Sanders took another long, slow sip from his coffee mug.

"No," he said. "You'll have to wait. We'll give you a call when we have an answer for you about the location of that Ms. Lucy character...but personally I don't think that he's a shman at all. He's more likely a catfish that knows how to use Photoshop."

"Just incase he's not, though? Will you trace the email anyway?" Jerry asked.

"Yea, of course. We'll get to it. Be patient."

That night, Jerry got in his large, silver SUV, and drove home to his apartment in

Edwards Town. Here there were a lot of paintings of fruit, flowers, landscapes, and classily nude men on the walls. Blank canvases were stacked into piles on the floor as were brushes, pallets, and tubes of unused paint.

Jerry stumbled through the door and into his apartment, groggy and exhausted from a day of being driven all over the place by a partially sober Conrad. The case was going badly. Jerry took his suit jacket of and threw it on the floor, then, his slacks and his underwear. Conrad was disobedient and distractible. Jerry walked into the bathroom, stared at himself in the mirror for a moment, and then, took a white bathrobe off of a hook on the wall and put it on. The Computer Department fuckers weren't ever going to call back. Jerry's old German Sheppard, Maximus, stood up on wobbly grey legs and staggered over to him, panting hard. And tomorrow Jerry would have to go back to The Company and do the whole fucking thing, basically all over again. Maximus pushed his cold, black nose against the hairy calf of Jerry's leg. Jerry felt the dog's moist tongue flick out over his skin and heard him bark once. Maximus' bark reminded Jerry of an old man's voice, deep and raspy.

Jerry knelt and pet the dog's brown head.

"Hello Maximus," He greeted him.

Jerry walked over to the tan, leather couch in the living room and sat down behind an easel that was set up in front of it. The easel held a blank canvas and there were a lot of paints and brushes laying on the couch and on the floor next to it. The dog jumped onto his lap, curled into a ball, and then, shut his eyes. Jerry thought about Lucy's riddle. Maybe if he could figure it out, he would be able to find Lucy without those computer fuckers.

The couch where Jerry was sitting was positioned with its back against a large, glass wall that looked out over Mantropolis City. Tall buildings were silhouetted against a purple sky as the sun began to sink low. Its eerie orange light illuminated Jerry's blank canvas.

Jerry picked up a brush and began to paint frantically. He had an image in his mind of Dionysus, the Greek God of debauchery. Tall and strong with flowing white robes. He was covered in grape vines and held a tall glass of wine in each massive hand. And his face...his face was jovial, Jerry decided, always smirking...no not smirking, *grinning*. Dionysus was grinning, and his eyes were crinkled from it. Jerry painted Dionysus's eyes as slits of blue. He painted his hair in short spiky strokes of dark, mustard blond.

When he was finished, Jerry put his brush down and stared at the painting. Quite contrary to his original intention, he had painted a grinning Conrad in white robes.

Jerry pulled the offending painting off of the easel and started again.

13

Days passed. The computer department

did not call. Frustrated, Jerry began calling the computer department every evening when he got home from work. Every night it was the same. Jerry would ask the guy on the phone if they had traced Lucy's email yet. The guy who answered the phone would put Jerry on hold for what seemed like two or three hours and then tell him that the email was on their "list" and they would get to it "eventually."

In the mornings, Jerry would meet up with Conrad and drive around to the homes and work places of Lucy's suspected followers. All of them were missing. All of them had disappeared suddenly, without any warning at all. Most had expressed some latent heterosexual tendencies or an interest in the

Strange Lands Lucy legend. Many kept illegal drawings and photographs of shmen in their homes. No real clues about Lucy's whereabouts emerged. Just the names of more suspicious people, and, with the names, new locations and people to question.

From time to time Jerry spoke with Danny Churchill, who despite his bizarre obsession with torture was really a very intelligent and reasonable man.

"To be honest, I was really a bit jealous of you and Conrad before," Churchill confided over lunch one afternoon. The two of them sometimes ate together in Churchill's office. It had started as a way for Jerry to avoid eating lunch with Conrad as often as possible but soon developed into a friendship between two somewhat odd, reclusive people, who fit badly with the mainstream.

"Jealous? Why in the world would you be jealous?" Jerry asked.

"He's an ex-boyfriend, actually," said Churchill. "Ah...I do still think about him sometimes, his grading, relentless stupidity, it was....*exquisite agony*. Perhaps it's not fair to call him an 'ex-boyfriend.' Conrad was never the relationship type. He wants what he can't have and after he's got it, he doesn't want it anymore. But I'll tell you something, Jerry, I've never met a man more adventurous in bed than Conrad Ryder. That man'll let you do basically *anything* to him."

"Gross. Too much information. Yea, Danny, Conrad and me are not going to sleep together," said Jerry. "We don't even like each other."

"He'll want to change that, I imagine," said Churchill.

"No really, he pisses me the fuck off," said Jerry.

"He won't give up until he's seduced you and he will seduce you. One way or another," said Churchill. "No man can resist Conrad Ryder. I've never seen him fail."

"Well, he's going to fail this time," said Jerry. "'Cause I ain't interested."

As time progressed, however, it became clear that what Churchill had said about Conrad was more or less accurate. He really did seem to be trying his best to get Jerry to like him. Since he'd learned that Jerry was a vegetarian, he had started bringing him whole heads of lettuce as a present.

"Here. This is for you," said Conrad, jumping over the driver's side door of his convertible and handing Jerry a whole head of lettuce.

Jerry took the lettuce out of Conrad's outstretched hand.

"What the fuck am I supposed to do with this?" he said, staring at the head of lettuce with incredulity, impatience, and disbelief.

"Yea...sorry, I usually apologize with food, but you hate food so....here's this crap," said Conrad.

"Thanks. I'll make a salad with it or something," said Jerry.

Then, sometimes, Conrad would tell Jerry stupid jokes.

"Hey, guess who would be an even better governor of Mantropolis than Governor Bert Wilhelm?" Conrad asked Jerry as they were speeding down the highway in his convertible one day.

Jerry sighed.

"No? Who would be a better governor of Mantropolis than Governor Bert Wilhelm?" Jerry repeated because he had the feeling that this was the set up to another of Conrad's stupid jokes.

"*My ball sack,*" said Conrad. His ball sack

was the punch line to literally all of his jokes. "Because *my ball sack* would be a better governor than him. Get it?"

Another day, while Conrad was stopped in the parking lot of a fast food joint with a greasy burger clutched in his large fist, he said:

"Do you know what's faster than the service here?"

"Let me think about this," said Jerry dryly. He took a bit of the whole head of lettuce that Conrad had brought him and chewed slowly as though contemplating Conrad's question. Jerry had heard enough of Conrad's jokes by this point to know the answer. He swallowed, then, finished: "Is the answer: *your ball sack*?"

Conrad laughed.

"Yea, how'd you know?" he said, grinning.

"Your ball sack is like....the only thing you ever talk about," said Jerry.

Days turned into months. Jerry gave up on hearing back from the computer department and had to accept that they either could not or would not trace Lucy's email. Instead, he started discussing Lucy's riddle with Conrad.

"She said the clue lives at the beginning and the end...at life and death. What do you think that means? Where do you think she's hiding?" Jerry asked.

Conrad opened his mouth to answer.

"And don't say she's in *your ball sack*," Jerry said quickly.

"What? She could be? I mean we've looked everywhere else right?" said Conrad.

"But what do you think it means? Life and death? Does she mean an executioner's chair that like...life prisoners being sent to the executioner's chair. Or does she mean the title of something. 'Life and Death'...like maybe there's a clue hidden somewhere and she's hidden it in a book entitled 'Life and Death? Or 'Beginning and End' or something like that?"

"It probably doesn't mean anything," said Conrad. "Shmen are supposed to be really stupid. Probably he was repeating something he heard that he thought sounded cool and it's just a bunch of nonsense."

"But Arnold Copperfield found her, so *he*

must have known what it meant," said Jerry.

"Maybe it's something that only someone who knew him would understand?" grunted Conrad. "I sure don't understand it."

In December, Jerry returned to his apartment one evening, and found Maximus staggering around, struggling to hold his sausage-like body up on four wobbly graying legs. Then, the German Sheppard's legs crumbled underneath of him and he vomited, before losing control of his bowels. He died in Jerry's lap in the car on the way to the vet, twitching hyperventilating, and foaming at the mouth. His death was not quick and clean like the fictional deaths of sainted television characters, but rather messy, agonizing, and gruesome as all death is in reality.

Jerry had the dog cremated and released his ashes in the lake under the bridge in Mantropolis Central Park. Then, overcome with the burden of a sudden and terrible loneliness, collapsed onto his knees and wept.

"He's in a better place, son," said Jerry's father, a man in his sixties with neatly parted white hair and a nose like a large bell.

"Do you really think the dirty lake in Mantropolis Park is a better place, Dad?" murmured Jerry. He was still sitting on the bridge, his face hidden in his knees.

"He's with Pops, Jerry," said Jerry's father, remembering his husband. He pictured the old man young again and running through a field with Maximus, the wind sweeping through his short auburn hair.   And then the old man wept: "In heaven. And they love you, Jerry. They're so p...proud of you."

"I love you, Dad," said Jerry quietly. Then, Jerry stood up and walked away.

Jerry stayed in his apartment for days after that. He stopped going to work. When the phone rang, he stared at it and let it ring.

After about five days of this, Jerry heard a knock on the front door of his apartment. He was quiet for a long time so that the person, whoever it was, would go away. The person kept knocking and knocking....and knocking.

"No one's here! Go away!" Jerry yelled in frustration.

"It's Conrad!" a deep voice on the other side of the door informed him.

"*Conrad*, go away!" Jerry yelled in frustration.

"I heard about what happened from your dad," said Conrad.

"When did you even find the time to talk to my dad, you fucking stalker?"

"When are you coming back to work? So your dog died? Go buy another dog!" said Conrad.

"I don't have the time to train another dog, Conrad! I have to go to work," shouted Jerry through the door in irritation.

"Then why don't you get a cat!" said Conrad.

"Because I don't want a cat, *Conrad!*," said Jerry.

"Why not?"

"Maybe because I don't want to come home to a pet that'll hiss and try to scratch my eyes out of my head when I try to *pet* it, *Conrad*!"

"Hold on, I'll be right back!" Conrad shouted through the door, and then, he darted off.

Jerry groaned and shook his head, hoping very much that Conrad would not come back.

A few hours passed and Jerry painted angry red and grey lines on a blank canvas, ripped the canvas off of his easel, and threw the hideous thing across the room in disgust.

He heard knocking on the front door

again.

"Jerry, it's Conrad!" Conrad shouted through the door. "Let me in."

"Go away, *Conrad!*" shouted Jerry angrily.

"I'm not leaving until you open the door," said Conrad.

"Fuck! Ok, fine! Let me just get dressed!" said Jerry.

Conrad waited for awhile, and then, he heard the lock on the door of Jerry's apartment click open. The door swung open and Jerry was standing there, wearing a mustard-stained white button down shirt and a pair of loose jeans. His usually neat hair was disheveled. His glasses were askew; his eyes obscured by the glare reflecting off of his thick lenses.

"I stopped by the birthing factory and got you a friend," said Conrad and he held up a small, brown, German Sheppard puppy. The puppy's mouth fell open and a long pink tongue fell out. Its little paws kicked in the air, looking for something solid to rest on.

Jerry extended his arms, took the puppy out of Conrad's hands, and held it against his body. The dog was warm, its tiny body soft and sausage-like. His little pointy tail flipped around and his pink tongue flopped out of his mouth as he began to pant. Jerry looked down at the dog in his arms. He couldn't help smiling at a creature so innocent.

"Thank you, Conrad," said Jerry after awhile. "He's beautiful."

"I'm glad you like him," said Conrad. "Well...I should be going now."

Jerry opened the door to his apartment the rest of the way and motioned inside.

"Stay," he murmured.

He walked back into the apartment. Conrad followed him.

"You want something to drink?" Jerry asked groggily.

Conrad stuck his hands in the pockets of his jeans and glanced around at the paintings on the walls as he walked.

"Got beer?" he asked.

Jerry had some red wine hidden in one of the cabinets of his kitchen but quickly decided against sharing this information with Conrad.

"I've got tea," Jerry said.

Conrad stopped in front of a few paintings of muscular, fair-haired men in varying stages of undress, near the entrance to the kitchen. Some of these men were dressed like Romans in white robes with wreaths laurels in their hair, some were nude and holding bowls of fruit. One had long, flowing hair and was riding a floating dolphin into the sunset. All had very similar faces and expressions.

"Are these me?" Conrad asked curiously, having noticed that the men in these pictures resembled him a great deal.

"No," said Jerry bluntly. He walked into the kitchen and prepared two cups of tea, then, walked back into the living room, holding two steaming cups on a tray in one hand, and the squirming puppy in the other. He saw that Conrad had already made himself at home on the sofa, as he was now sitting on it like he owned it, with his elbows resting on the top of the chair's back and his knees apart.

"Did you paint all these?" he asked Jerry.

"Yea," said Jerry. He set the tea tray down on the coffee table. Then, he sat down on the couch as far away from Conrad as it was possible to sit. Then, he put the puppy down in his lap. The dog curled itself into a ball and fell asleep. Jerry stroked his furry head and velvet ears slowly.

"I like them," said Conrad.

"What?"

"The paintings. I like them," said Conrad.

"Oh," said Jerry. "Thank you."

There was silence for a moment. The dog in Jerry's lap breathed in and out slowly. His tiny black nose made a quiet whistling sound and his velvet ears twitched once.

"You're a really weird dude, aren't you?" said Conrad to Jerry after awhile.

"Yea. I guess I am," said Jerry quietly.

"But it's not always a bad thing to be different," Conrad mused, sounding far away. "You're not like anyone I've ever met before, Jerry."

"Conrad, I assure you. I'm *exactly* like everyone you've ever met before," said Jerry.

"No you're not," Conrad teased.

"*Yes.* I am," Jerry replied promptly, getting irritated.

"Can I kiss you?" Conrad asked.

"*No,*" Jerry replied bluntly.

"I know I was busting your balls at first. But I never worked with an agent who had a higher rank than me before. It kind of pissed me off," Conrad laughed.

"Oh. Did it? I didn't notice," Jerry lied. He picked a steaming cup off of the tea tray, raised it to his lips, and took a sip.

"How did you get such a high rank, anyway?" Conrad asked. "You said you were in the office until this case."

"Yea, I was," said Jerry. "But it's no big deal really. They award you rank points for learning skills."

"Then you must have all kinds of skills," said Conrad, grinning.

"Yea."

"What kinds of skills?"

"Medical mostly. It was all for the pay raise, since I never thought I'd see the field," said Jerry. "I learned how to clean and mend bullet and stab wounds. CPR. That kind of thing."

"Really. I never knew that about you. You must be super smart," said Conrad.

Jerry laughed.

"No," he said, shaking his head. "It's really pretty easy. I could teach you sometime, if you want."

"I would like that," said Conrad. Then, he

lifted the remaining cup off of the tea tray and drank down its contents like it was one of his bears.

It was quiet for a moment. The dog snorted in his sleep. The air conditioner made a buzzing sound as it sprang to life.

"*So*....TV?" Conrad inquired cautiously.

"Yea, TV," said Jerry and he picked up the remote and turned on the large, flat screen television mounted on the wall across from where they sat.

Part 2: The Surrogate Incubator

Room

1

Conrad often came over Jerry's apartment

to watch sports and action movies after that.

Jerry wasn't sure if it was because Conrad liked

him or if he liked *his* TV. It was probably a little of both.

The dog got older. His floppy ears perked up and his legs grew long. Jerry had named him Dionysus. Dio for short.

"Dio, sit!" Jerry said to the dog. The dog's large pink tongue fell out of his mouth and Jerry fed him a piece of bacon. "Dio, lay down." The dog laid down. Jerry fed him a piece of bacon. "Dio, bang bang!" Jerry said making a gun with his hand and aiming it at the dog. The dog rolled around on the floor and kicked his legs in the air. Jerry fed him another piece of bacon.

"Yea, explosions! Alright!" Conrad cheered. Per usual, he was sitting on Jerry's tan leather couch, watching something on television.

He had a plate of bacon on his lap and a beer in his hand. A large mushroom cloud exploded on the television screen. CG fire and chunks of debris were blown across an imaginary city. A large, buff, shirt-less black man with camo pants and a machine gun screamed: "It's a testoster-splosion! Everybody *get down!*"

"*Christ*, is that Testosterone Tyrone?" Jerry groaned, grinning.

"Everybody get down! It's a *testoster-splosion!*" Conrad and Jerry both exclaimed and then they both laughed

"Testosterone levels are at an all time high!" Testosterone Tyrone screamed from the television set. Testosterone Tyrone had only one volume: screaming. "Gratuitous nudity is imminent! Awesome-ite laser head sharks are being torpedoed at us by the enemy camp, Mr. President! The giant robots have taken the grand floor of the White House! *Brace for impact!*"

Giant, marching CG robots appeared on the screen of the television. Metal sharks with red laser beams shooting out of their eyes flew toward the screen. Testosterone Tyrone shot his machine guns at them and blew them up one at a time. He kept shooting for a good five or six minutes straight but never seemed to run out of bullets.

"This is the part they put in for the 3-D" said Conrad, stuffing his mouth with a fist full of bacon.

"No shit," said Jerry. "Hey is this

Testosterone Tyrone 2: This Time With Balls, or Testosterone Tyrone 3: Bigger, Manlier, and Uncut?"

"It's Testosterone Tyrone 4: Tyrone vs. Mantastic Mantuala," said Conrad.

Jerry snorted in mock derision.

"They made a fourth one?"

"Of course," said Conrad.

"It'll be a cold day in hell, when you out man me, Mantastic Mantuala!" Testosterone Tyrone screamed from the television, and then, he spouted one of his famous catch phrases: "Real men eat grenades for lunch and fart explosions!"

"This is so dumb," Jerry snorted, laughing.

The movie cut to commercial.

"Next on the Dude-BRO channel," a deep-voiced announcer proclaimed from the television set: *"The Indestructible Man*, followed by *Not Without My Nunchucks."*

The phone rang. Jerry walked over to the kitchen and picked it off of the counter.

"Hello," he said, holding the phone up to his ear.

"Yea, Jerry Cosco?" the voice on the other end of the phone asked.

"That's me."

"This is Carl Sanders with the Company Computer department."

"Hello Carl."

"We've traced the location of your Ms. Lucy, or the location of the computer he sent the email from at least," said Sanders.

"That's great news," said Jerry. "Where was it sent from?"

"2298, Corigan Avenue. Lamerts Ville, Mantropolis State," said Sanders.

"Anything else I should know?" Jerry asked.

"No that's about it," said Sanders.

"Thank you," said Jerry.

"You're welcome."

"Bye."

"Good bye."

Jerry hung up.

"Conrad, get up! We're going to 2298, Corigan Avenue!" Jerry shouted, grabbing his suit jacket from a hook on the wall by the door.

"Corigan Avenue? That's where my old partner used to live," Conrad murmured. His muscles tensed and his expression shifted from relaxed to apprehensive. Conrad rose from the sofa slowly and moved with a slow, brooding reluctance that was very uncharacteristic of him.

2

Conrad was silent as he raced down the road, weaving around cars that weren't speeding fast enough, through red lights, stop signs, and median strips; knocking over orange cones. Jerry stared straight ahead with wide, unblinking eyes and gripped the armrests of his seat, as though this would do something to protect him in the event of a crash.

"Ms. Lucy's email was sent from

Mantropolis State," said Jerry, pointing to the sign on the left side of the road, denoting an exit. "Take a left at that sign up ahead."

Conrad shook his head.

"Too slow," he grunted. "I know a short cut."

He swerved and took a sharp turn right, shooting down a different exit with unnecessary speed. The black cement road became patchy, broken, and grey. Eventually it gave way to loose gravel. The tall buildings on either side of them became dilapidated, graffiti-covered row homes with overgrown yards.

"Uh...Conrad....are you sure this is the right way?" Jerry inquired, beginning to get worried.

"Sure it is," said Conrad confidently, "Probably. Anyway, this way's faster."

"Are you sure?

"Sure I'm sure," said Conrad.

"I mean....we should have been there like ten minutes ago..."

"Trust me, this is better—Oh my holy crap, It's a lasagna cart!" Conrad shouted, pointing ahead into the distance. A white cart with a picture of a happy, smiling slab of lasagna on it, sat on the side of the road. A handsome Italian man in a white sleeveless shirt was standing next to it, jumping around and Twirling a sign with the words "Lasagna Cart!!!" printed on it in bold, black letters.

"No. We're not stopping." said Jerry

exasperatedly. "This is *off task*."

"Oh, we're stopping," said Conrad.

"No. We're not."

"That lasagna," said Conrad pointing to the approaching lasagna cart again. "*Has a face. We're stopping.*"

"No, Conrad. No we're not."

"Yes. Yes we are."

"No we aren't."

"Yes."

"*No.*"

"Yes."

"NO!"

"Yes."

"Conrad, I am your superior officer and we are not wasting time on that stupid lasagna cart!" shouted Jerry.

Conrad pulled his car over on the side of the road, next to the lasagna cart, and parked. Then, he jumped over the driver's side door and jogged up to the Italian man holding the sign.

"Yea, what's the baconsagna?" asked Conrad, glancing over at the paper menu at the top of the cart.

"That's a bunch of bacon wrapped in a lasagna shell that is just more bacon, signore," said the Italian man.

"Perfect. I'll take five of those, no *six* — and a large soda — and like twelve of those little plastic cup things filled with tomatoe sauce," said Conrad. Then, he glanced back at Jerry and called out. "Do you want anything?"

"No!" Jerry called back. He had his arms crossed and looked severely pissed off.

"Nothing for him," said Conrad to the Italian man.

"Oh," said the Italian man. "I have, like....not that much bacon in my cart. Why don't you wait here while I go get more?"

The Italian man jogged away and into the distance, disappearing from sight.

"Great. Just Perfect," complained Jerry. "Now he's gone."

"Meh...I can wait for him to come back," said Conrad indifferently.

A few moments passed and the proprietor of the lasagna cart did not return.

"Agh! This sucks!" Jerry shouted,

jumping out of the car and slamming the door behind him.

"Relax, he said he'd be right back," said Conrad.

A black car pulled over on the side of the road and parked behind Conrad's convertible. The doors opened and two men jumped out.

"...Oh no," Jerry moaned under his breath.

The man on the right was tall and pale with slicked back black hair. He wore a black leather jacket with a striped purple and black tie. The man on the left was taller, darker and more muscular with a shiny bald head. He wore an identical outfit but with a black and purple striped bow tie and the sleeves ripped off of his leather jacket.

Jerry walked over to Conrad and tapped him on the shoulder.

Conrad turned toward the two men. Head bowed, fists raised, muscles tensed.

"Uh, Conrad," Jerry mumbled. "I think we should get out of here."

A second black car pulled up and parked, blocking Conrad's car from the left side. Two more men jumped out, one with spiky black hair and a purple and black striped shirt under his leather jacket, and one with a tall black and yellow Mohawk. The man with the Mohawk was shirtless and had the words "PROPERTY OF MASCHIO" tattooed across his chest in purple letters.

"This is Maschio's land," said the bald

one. His voice was deep and low like scraping gravel. "All trespassers must pay a fee."

"We're Company Men," said Conrad gruffly.

"Everyone says that," said the bald one.

"No, really, we are," Jerry said, pointing to The Company's insignia, which was embroidered on to the left shoulder of his blue button-down shirt.

"We are properdy of Maschio!" said the spiky haired one. He spoke with a severe speech impediment as his tongue was pierced by several silver rings. "We do not fear the governdmentd! Maschio is righdtful lord!"

The other followers of Maschio shouted their approval.

"What are your demands?" asked Conrad grimly.

"Firstly, acknowledge that Lord Maschio is the most *fabulous* and well-dressed mafia drug lord in all of Mantropolis! No Manazonian is a match for him in brains, power, muscle, or fashion sense."

"Fine. Maschio is the most fabulous drug lord in Mantropolis. He's the greatest." Conrad growled.

"Secondly, we will take all of your money and your car," continued the bald one. "And thirdly, Lord Maschio has taken a shine to your little boyfriend. He will have his way with him tonight! What say you, Company Man? Will you give Maschio the toll he requires, or will you die?"

The followers of Maschio each pulled a switch blade from his sleeve and clicked it open. In one quick, decisive motion, Conrad pulled the gun from his belt and shot the bald one square between the eyes. Maschio's remaining servants charged at Conrad with their knives drawn.

Conrad punched the one with the Mohawk in the face just as the other man was about to impale him through the throat with his switch blade. The henchman was smaller than Conrad and fell easily, crumpling into an unconscious pile on the ground at Conrad's feet. In the next instant, Conrad turned around and kicked the one with the slicked back hair's legs out from under him, just before the henchman was able to stab him in the back with his switch blade.

While this was happening, the one with the spiky hair ran toward Jerry with his knife drawn. Jerry raised his gun quickly and shot the man through the face, blowing his brains out through the back of his head. The spiky haired henchmen's legs crumbled underneath of him and he fell; now a bloody pile of black leather and purple stripes at Jerry's feet.

A pair of shiny, tan, men with long black hair and muscular arms popped out from the two trunks of Maschio's two black cars. They looked like twin brothers and each one wielded a buzzing black and purple stun gun.

The twins charged at Conrad (who had

his back turned to them and was not aware of their presence), quickly, their large feet surprisingly quiet, as they fell against patches of sparse lawn and loose gravel.

"Conrad, watch out!" Jerry shouted, aiming his gun at one of the twins. The twin was too far away to guarantee an accurate shot and too close to Conrad to grantee that Conrad wouldn't be taking the bullet instead.

Conrad turned quickly, and aimed his gun at one of the charging twins. He aimed for the head but missed badly and shot the man's ankle instead, just as the second twin accelerated, jumped into the air, and electrocuted Conrad's large, thick neck with the stun gun. Conrad yelled and his body convulsed with electricity. He grabbed the henchman by his throat and started choking him. The electricity surged through Conrad's body into the henchman's and now they were both being electrocuted. But the henchman kept his hand on the trigger of the stun gun and the stun gun pressed tight against Conrad's throat. Both men fell down unconscious.

The twin who had been shot in the ankle started limping toward Jerry, stun gun raised.

"Maschio will have his prize," the remaining twin growled, advancing slowly, his head bowed, his eyes masked in shadow.

Jerry raised his gun, aimed it at the henchman's head and pulled the trigger. Nothing happened. Jerry's expression shifted from one of stoic calm to one of panic. He clicked the trigger on the gun several times in rapid succession. Nothing happened. The henchman grinned. He continued to advance slowly. Jerry dropped the gun and put his hands in the air.

"Wait!" he shouted calmly. "Take me to Maschio!"

The twin lowered his stun gun but continued to advance. Jerry put his arms down.

"I'll go willingly!" he announced. He glanced down at Conrad who was unconscious on the ground with the unconscious twin on top of him. "Just make sure no harm comes to me or my partner....Let's Maschio and I discuss this like gentlemen."

3

Maschio's remaining henchman blindfolded Jerry, and then, the unconscious Conrad. After that, they dumped them in the trunk of one black car. Jerry felt the car begin to move. He felt Conrad's lungs expand and decompress slowly underneath of him. The larger man's limbs were twisted awkwardly to fit in the trunk and his massive body left little room for Jerry, who was now feeling very uncomfortable, face pressed flat against the car's plastic interior.

Jerry's brain swelled and churned with disorienting panic. *They're going to kill me.* He thought. *I've only got until Maschio's grown bored of me and God knows that won't take long.*

174

The car's engine revved, and Jerry felt it take a sharp turn right, as the top of his head was smashed against the side of the trunk. Conrad groaned quietly and his body twitched. Jerry prayed silently that he wouldn't regain consciousness, and then, realized how stupid that was and prayed silently that he *would* regain consciousness. Conrad had a much better chance of taking out Maschio with brute force than Jerry had of convincing Maschio not to kill them with words.

Jerry felt the car stop. Then, the heavy footfalls of Maschio's henchman as he limped slowly toward the back of the car.

4

"I have returned, Lord Maschio, with the

prize you requested," growled Maschio's henchman. He led a blindfolded Jerry by the arm.

"Okay, then," Maschio congratulated him. Jerry couldn't see him through the blind fold but his voice was very harsh and Italian mobster like. "Bring him in here!"

Maschio's henchman led Jerry forward into a room. Then, untied his blindfold. It slipped off of his face and he blinked several times both confused by what he was looking at and disoriented by the sudden blinding rush of light. As his eyes adjusted, he saw that he was in a classy, well furnished room. The walls were painted red and trimmed in dark molding. An intricately carved antique mahogany table was dressed in a red table cloth and set for two. A line of men, holding long serrated swords, who wore black leather jackets and purple and black striped shirts, stood in a line behind a larger man. The larger man wore a long purple leather cloak with a high collar. Jerry blinked again. The man in the purple leather coat's face came into sharper focus. He was a muscular Italian man with a goatee, thick shiny dark hair, and handsome, chiseled features. He sat in the chair, facing Jerry, looking almost disinterested as he sipped red wine from a tall crystal glass.

"You're Maschio?" Jerry asked, sounding confused.

"I am Maschio," the man replied and then he motioned to the chair across from him.

"Please. Sit."

Jerry sat down in the chair across from Maschio. Then, he squinted.

"Are you...the man from the lasagna cart?" Jerry asked in confusion.

"Indeed, that was I, Maschio, cleverly disguised to avoid detection, signore," said Maschio.

"Huh. Who knew that the great Maschio dances in front of his own lasagna cart." Jerry mused.

"What can I say, signore. Sometimes the best place to hide is in plain sight, ay?" said Maschio with a sage wink. He lifted a bottle of wine and filled Jerry's tall crystal glass. "Please. Have some wine."

"Uh...no thank you. I don't really drink,"
Jerry replied nervously.

"You've done a job on my henchmen,
Company man. I must say. I am impressed.
What is your name?" Maschio asked.

"...Jerry Cosco," Jerry replied reluctantly.

"Jerry Cosco, sei molt bello. I'm quite
smitten . I will have my way with you tonight,
ay?" Maschio informed him.

"Ah hahah....uhh...what kind of a guy do
you think I am?" Jerry chuckled nervously,
shrinking away from the larger man. "At least
let me buy you dinner first."

"Ha ha haha haha...." Maschio laughed
back. "You're a charmer, Jerry Cosco."

"Right um....so this is pretty awkward.

I've come here to negotiate with you but let's just say...for uh...for the sake of argument that sex is off of the table?"

"Sex is on the table, signore. Sex is on every table," said Maschio.

"Right um...yeah...trying to finish my sentence, here. So, let's say, for the sake of argument, that sex is off the table," Jerry began again.

"On the table," Maschio interrupted.

"Off," Jerry corrected.

"On."

"Off."

"On."

"I'm speaking figuratively here, Maschio. So, let's say, for the sake of argument, that sex...uh.....is not part of the deal. Is there anyway that you might agree to let my partner and me go?" Jerry asked cautiously.

"Why, signore, if I did'nt know any better, I would say that you are attempting to rebuke my advances," said Maschio, starting to sound suspicious.

"Uh....," Jerry faltered, at a loss for words. This was exactly what he was doing.

"Jerry," Maschio said, grinning. "One way or another....I always get what I want."

"Yes...right...um...," Jerry stumbled. A gleaming silver crucifix on a short silver chain around Maschio's neck caught his eye and he stopped talking. The necklace gave him an idea.

"A lesser man would be insulted, Jerry,"

said Maschio, sounding insulted. "There are men who would saw off their left nut for the opportunity that I am giving you now."

"No...uh...you miss understand," lied Jerry. "It's not that I wouldn't like to...you are a very handsome and powerful man, obviously. To sleep with you would be an honor. But Maschio, you have to understand, I am very religious...and my husband....well....he......he's very jealous."

"Your husband?"

"Yes," lied Jerry. "You see I would sleep with you, but I'm trying to be faithful to my husband here. And then, of course, there's Jesus to think about, me being a very religious man... and everything."

"Indeed, signore," said Maschio, touching the silver crucifix around his neck with his free hand. His other hand still held the wine glass, periodically lifting it to his parted lips. "I too am very devoted to our holy father. I respect your conviction, Jerry. Your husband is a lucky man."

"Thank you, Maschio," said Jerry.

"So let's agree then that sex is off of the tables...and the floors, and the beds, and the counters, and so forth....," said Maschio.

"Thank you, Maschio," Jerry said. "I hope you understand that my marriage is very important to me."

"Jerry....," Maschio crooned almost lovingly. "You must not think that I am a bad person...just because I sell drugs and have many sex slaves."

"No, no. Of course not," lied Jerry.

"Your partner killed several of my men. He is the beloved son of the two highest ranking officials in The Company. Now that he is my captive, I will hold him for ransom," said Maschio. He pulled the lid off of a silver tray at the center of the table, revealing a pile of bacon shaped to look like slabs of lasagna and drizzled with tomatoes sauce.

"Please," Maschio said. "Have a baconsagna."

"Uh....no thanks. I'm not hungry," Jerry lied, eyeing the bacon lasagnas suspiciously. Perhaps they were drugged.

"Suit yourself," said Maschio.

"For the sake of argument, if you were to hold Conrad for ransom, what would you ask for him?" Jerry asked.

Maschio grabbed a bacon lasagna from the top of the pile and shoved it into his mouth, crunching loudly as he contemplated this. He swallowed, and then, answered: "I would ask for money, of course, and then, I would ask for a high ranking position in the government, to have a law passed, which would make it illegal for all people to sell cocaine, except for me. And then, I would ask for a few surrogate incubators from the birthing factory, to make as many sons as I wanted, in the forbidden way. And then I would ask for the blood of Ferraro Inglacius, The Company's Arch Director of Justice

---

185

Enforcement, so that I would have something to give up in the negotiations."

"And what would you do if The Company refused to pay your price in exchange for Conrad?" Jerry inquired darkly.

Maschio took a long, slow sip from his glass of wine.

"Then, Jerry," he said. "I would torture him until he begged The Company to pay his ransom. And if I still did not get my ransom, I would cut off his toes and fingers one at a time, and send them to his fathers in a box. And if I still did not get my ransom, I would kill him and be done with the thing."

"Jesus."

"Do not say the lord's name in vain,

Jerry," said Maschio.

"Sorry, I meant *gee wiz*," Jerry corrected himself.

"Tell me about your husband," Maschio inquired conversationally. There was a bit of a jealous glint in his eye. Perhaps he was already plotting the murder of Jerry's imaginary husband.

Jerry made up a story fast.

"My husband's name is Bob," lied Jerry. "We met in church. He was a florist for awhile but after we adopted a few baby boys from the birthing factory he quit and now he's a stay-at-home-dad."

"Do you love your children, Jerry?"

"Please. Leave them out of this."

"Well, do you?"

"I do, yes. With all of my heart."

"Ah. Your husband is a lucky man," said Maschio. "You are a family man; a provider. I respect that. Signore, I will not suffer a man such as yourself to spend the night in the cage with my ransom boy, like a prisoner. Please, stay with me in my guest room. You are my guest here."

"Thanks, but I think I'll stick with Conrad tonight," said Jerry.

"You would sleep on the steel floor of a cage instead of in the fine, down comforter of my bed?"

"If Conrad is doing it. Then, so can I," said Jerry.

"If Conrad jumped off a cliff would you follow him?"

"Yea, probably."

Maschio finished his meal. Jerry watched him, quietly, not daring to reach across the table and grab one of the bacon lasagnas off of the tray.

There was something dangerous about that look in Maschio's eyes. Something that Jerry did not like at all.

"Good night, Jerry. It's been a pleasure," Maschio said. Then, one of Maschio's men slipped the blindfold back over Jerry's eyes and led him away again.

5

Conrad opened his eyes slowly. His head

ached. His face was pressed against something flat and cold.

"Ughh....," he groaned deeply. He was disoriented but his vision was returning to him slowly. He saw now that the floor underneath of him was metal. Then, he tried to move his arms but found that his wrists were tied together behind his back. He groaned again and rolled over onto his side. Vertical steel bars confronted him, and beyond that, a dark, empty room.

An hour passed. Conrad struggled to free himself but was unsuccessful. He tried to stand up but found that his ankles were bound tightly with rope. His head ached. The ropes chafed the skin on his wrists and ankles and cut off the circulation in his hands and feet. He noticed a flickering light bulb in the distance. It dangled from a stripped wire in the ceiling, periodically illuminating a steel door and a few tall piles of wooden crates.

The steel door swung open. A blindfolded Jerry was led into the room by one of Maschio's purple and black clad henchmen. The henchman walked Jerry to Conrad's cage, unlocked the cage door, shoved Jerry inside, and then, locked the cage behind him again. He did this quickly and wordlessly, then, turned and exited the room.

Jerry untied the blindfold over his eyes and threw it down on the floor in disgust, glaring at Conrad as he did so. Conrad stared back from the floor, through squinting eyes.

"God damn it, Conrad!" Jerry shouted, pointing a finger accusingly at Conrad. "This is *your* fault!"

Jerry paused as though anticipating a response. Conrad did not answer.

"This happened because you had to stop at that lasagna stand, even though, *I*, your superior officer, told you specifically not to! And now they're going to hold you for ransom and torture you and Maschio's going to rape me and probably tattoo his name to my forehead or some shit and you know why? Because this is *OFF TASK*! Off task. Off task. OFF TASK! OFF! *TASK!*" Jerry raved, waving his hands around wildly in his frustration. He was starting to hyperventilate, "We couldn't be farther away from *the task*! If the task was on the other side of this stupid planet! And we're all the way over here with this irrelevant FUCKING *OFF TASK* SHIT! Aaaaghhhh!" Jerry punched the bars of the cage in his frustration, badly bruising his knuckle. "*FUCK!*"

"...Did you know that you jump up and down and wave your arms around like a maniac when you're angry?" moaned Conrad groggily.

"Conrad, *shut up*."

"It's true," Conrad groaned. "And your face gets red like a tomato. You look like a fuckin' idiot."

"I *hate* you."

Both men were quiet for a moment. The distant light bulb flickered and buzzed. Conrad rolled onto his back and stared up at the ceiling of the cage.

"Listen, Jerry," he said. "I'm sorry."

"You're......*huh*?" Jerry repeated quietly. This had not been the response he was expecting.

"You're right. This is my fault. And there's a good chance that Maschio is going to kill us both now," said Conrad.

Jerry sat down on the floor next to Conrad.

"Do you really think he's going to kill us?"

"Well he's not going to let us go," said Conrad.

"Well not me, anyway" Jerry said. "I've seen his face now. He still might let you go, though. If the company pays your ransom."

"Did he mention what he would ask them for?" Conrad asked grimly.

"Money. A position of power in the government. The blood of one of his enemies. Surrogate incubators," Jerry replied, counting the things off on his fingers.

"Surrogate incubators. Huh. They won't give him those. I'm probably worth the rest."

"...Yea....but why is that, do you think?" Jerry mused darkly.

"The Company doesn't give surrogate incubators to anybody," explained Conrad. "I've never even seen one. Shit, dude, I couldn't even tell you what one looks like."

"Really? Your dads never let you see the

inside of the birthing factory?" Jerry asked curiously.

"No, why? Have yours?"

"No. But I thought since your dads are such important people that you might have seen it," said Jerry.

"Nah. I've only heard of it," mused Conrad, crossing his arms and leaning forward over his scrunched up knees. "But I've never been inside. Only people who work there can go inside."

"Do you think that it's really as grim as those Lucy sympathizers say?"

"Eh. Who knows?"

"You know I've always wanted to see inside the factory," Jerry confessed with a sigh.

"It's one of the reasons I became a Company man. I guess I'll never get to do that now I'm about to die, though."

"I wish you had told me," said Conrad. "We've got clearance to go pretty much anywhere we want while we're on this Lucy case."

Jerry turned his head and looked at Conrad who was now staring ahead into the distance.

"Really? Even the factory?" Jerry asked. "I thought that 'everywhere' just meant everywhere except the factory."

"Yea, I think even the factory. But I didn't mention it because I didn't really wanna go there."

"Really? Why not? Don't you want to know where babies come from? I want to know where babies come from," said Jerry excitedly.

"Yea, I'm curious and everything. But I was thinking...maybe we're better off not knowing?"

"Don't you like babies?"

"Sure. I don't have a problem with babies," said Conrad. "It's just, you know. Maybe there's a reason that we're not supposed to know."

"Do you think it's true that a stork brings them from a far away place and then drops them into the top of the factory for sorting?"

"Mn...maybe. I'm not smart enough to understand these things. So I guess, probably that but more...sciencey? Maybe?"

"Or do you think that they grow in the centers of cabbages and that the factory is really just one gigantic cabbage patch, filled with cabbage babies?" mused Jerry curiously.

"Ok that one makes sense. So when Roy said that the surrogate incubators have their heads and limbs circumcised, he was talking about pruning heads of lettuce or something, and the extra limbs that grow off the sides of it?" said Conrad.

"Yea, that sounds about right. Ok then. Mystery solved. I guess I can stop being curious about it now," said Jerry, grinning. He stood up quickly. "But wait, that gives me an idea."

"Ok," said Conrad, glancing up at him.

"What is it?"

"Maschio wants a surrogate incubator, right? And the company won't give him one," said Jerry.

"Yea."

"But that doesn't mean that he can't get one," said Jerry. "Because we're Company Men and we can go into the factory and get one for him ourselves."

"That won't work," said Conrad.

"No, it will," insisted Jerry. "Listen, we can take a surrogate incubator from the factory and say that we're bringing it back to The Company lab to examine it for evidence. Lucy was the 'result of a botched factory process'…so this should work. We might even find some very *on task* clues while we're poking around the factory. Then, we're 'intercepted' on our way from the birthing factory to The Company by Maschio's henchmen. They steal the incubator. It's not our fault because, hey they're criminals. That's what they do. And in exchange for this 'accident' as well as, of course, me keeping my mouth shut about his identity, Maschio releases us and spares us both our lives."

"Yea," said Conrad, grinning. "That could work!"

"He won't trust us enough to agree to it though," mused Jerry.

"But what if he has collateral or something," said Conrad.

"Like what kind of collateral?"

"I don't know. Why don't you ask him when you see him again?"

"Right. And when do you think that will be? He might not even talk to us directly again. He might just send his henchmen in here to deal with us from now on.

The door of the room opened again and one of Maschio's purple and black clad henchmen entered the room.

"Lord Maschio has been watching you from the security cameras," the man informed them. "He has sent me to inform you that he is interested in your deal."

"Oh." Jerry said, sounding surprised. "Really?"

"That's great," said Conrad.

Maschio's henchman reached into the pocket of his purple leather pants and withdrew a vibrating cell phone. He tapped the screen of the cell phone with his thumb and put it up to his ear.

"Yea. Uhuh. Ok," said the henchman into the phone.

He lowered the phone and said: "Maschio will release both of you in exchange for one surrogate incubator from the birthing factory. To ensure that you do not double cross him, he will have both of you drink The Alpha B-47 neurotoxin."

"The *what*?" Jerry inquired skeptically.

"This is a poison, which lays dormant in the body for 12 hours with no effect and then travels to the brain, causing a slow and agonizing death," explained Maschio's henchman. "The Alpha B-47 neurotoxin is a mixture of a variety of several different neurotoxins possessed by The Company. Only Lord Maschio knows which neurotoxins they are, however, and so only Lord Maschio can provide you with the antidote. Cross him and you will die from the poison's effects. Deliver him the surrogate incubator and you will receive the antidote. Maschio gets his surrogate incubator. You get your freedom. That is the deal."

"That's my kind of deal!" Conrad blurted out. "Let's do it!"

Jerry glared at Conrad, hoping to shut

him up. However, it was no use.

"Tell him, *we'll do it*!" Conrad boomed enthusiastically.

"Okay, I will tell Maschio that you will take his deal," said the henchman. He picked up the cell phone again and said something to Maschio in Italian. Then, he turned toward the two captives and said: "Domani, *tomorrow*, you get Maschio his surrogate incubator *or die*."

And with those words, he exited the room. The metal door made a loud slamming sound as it snapped shut behind him.

"What the fuck, Conrad?" Jerry shouted, clawing at his disheveled auburn hair anxiously. "We were supposed to *negotiate*! Now we have to trust Maschio not to let us die from poison!"

"Yea, but at least he has to let us go to get his surrogate incubator," said Conrad.

"We could have negotiated a better deal, *Conrad*," Jerry growled, drawing his eye brows together with distain.

"Yea, no we couldn't have," growled Conrad and his face contorted to match Jerry's disdainful expression.

"Yea, Conrad. We could have. I am very good at *negotiating!*"

"Ooh look at me, I'm so good at *negotiating!*" Conrad mocked, raising his deep voice an octave. "What do you want a fuckin' cookie?"

"Yea, Conrad. I want a fucking cookie. So that I can ram it down your throat and *choke you to death* with it!" Jerry shouted.

"Fatherfucker, you couldn't take me in a fight if I had my arms tied behind my back and you were holding a grenade launcher!" Conrad boasted loudly. "That's probably why you're the worst Company Man there is and everybody fucking hates you!"

The room was quiet for a moment. The distant light bulb flickered and buzzed. Jerry stared at the light bulb and frowned. The yellow glare reflecting off of his large glasses masked his eyes.

"You know what...," Jerry said after awhile. "It doesn't make any sense to fight about this. What's done is done. And what will happen, will happen. We're in this together. So we might as well make the best of it."

"Are you trying to negotiate with me?" Conrad muttered.

"Yea. Is it working?"

"Maybe, a little bit."

"Tomorrow we'll have to work together or die," continued Jerry. "Or work together *and* die. One of those two things. Either way, our odds of success are much better if we don't fight with each other about stupid shit."

"Ok," conceded Conrad. "It's hard to argue with that."

Conrad's eyes closed slowly and he drifted off to sleep. He began to snore loudly. Jerry laid down on the floor and stared up at the shiny metal surface that was the top of the cage.

He could see his reflection there, staring back at him. *....If you say her name three times in the mirror after midnight, she'll jump out from behind the glass and bite your penis off,* Roy's voice echoed in Jerry's mind.

"Strange Lands Lucy," Jerry whispered quietly to himself, staring up at the ceiling of the cage. "....Strange Lands Lucy........*Strange Lands Lucy....*"

Jerry waited for a moment as though expecting something to happen. Nothing did. Jerry closed his eyes and fell asleep with a grin on his face. Chubby infants being carried in the mouths of storks and sprouting from the centers of leafy green cabbage heads haunted his dreams.

6

In the morning, a couple of Maschio's men entered the room where Conrad and Jerry were being held captive. These men were not dressed in the flamboyant black and purple outfit that marked them as Maschio's followers, however. They were dressed in civilian clothes: jeans, sneakers, and button down flannel shirts.

The henchman on the left was dark haired and tall. He had a cell phone pressed to his ear and was speaking to someone on the other line in rapid Italian. The henchman on the right had white blond hair and a dark goatee. He carried two vials of green liquid. One in either hand.

"Maschio says you must drink the neurotoxin before we release you," the dark haired one said, lowering his cell phone.

"Then, we will blindfold you both and take you far away from this location," said the blond one.

"From here you go to the birthing factory, retrieve the surrogate incubator, and deliver it to the black car parked out in front of the Stay Late Motel on the corner of Arrow and Eighth Street. Do this in under twelve hours and you will receive the antidote," said the dark haired one.

"Fail and you will die," said the blond one.

"Stop it, *stop interrupting!*" the dark haired one snapped turning toward the blond one.

"What? I thought we were doing a thing," said the Blond one, sounding confused.

"Well we're not doing *a thing*," growled the dark haired one. "I tell them the mission. You stand there menacingly and don't say anything. That's our thing. That's what we do."

"But I was thinking we could try a new thing," said the blond one innocently.

"Oh, God damn it, Fernando! We're not doing a new thing! You make me look like a freakin' idiot in front of these guys!"

The dark haired one turned toward Conrad and Jerry and added: "Now drink the neurotoxin—"

"Or we will kill you," said Fernando, taking a gun out of his pocket and pointing it at Conrad's head. Jerry recognized the gun as his own.

"Oh my freakin' God, Fernando! Shut the fuck up! You *ruined* it!" the dark haired one shouted in frustration.

"Sorry, I thought we were doing a thing, Lorenzo," said Fernando innocently.

"God damn it, I told you already we're not doing the thing!" Lorenzo shouted in frustration his accent got much stronger when he was angry. "I talk. You don't say anything. That's our thing. That's what we do!"

Fernando nodded silently and held the two vials of green liquid out in front of him.

"Now, drink. Both of you." Lorenzo ordered.

Fernando stuck his hands through the bars of the cage so that Jerry could grab the vials of liquid. Jerry stared at the ominous green liquid for a moment but did not touch it. One of them was much more full than the other.

"You are smaller so you drink less," Fernando said to Jerry. He spoke quietly, in hopes that Lorenzo would not notice him talking.

Jerry reached a hand out and grabbed the less-full vial of green liquid. Then, tipped it into his mouth and quickly swallowed its contents. Then, he took the second vial of green liquid out of Fernando's hand, walked over to Conrad and poured its contents into his open mouth. Conrad choked and wheezed, hunching forward as though he were about to spit it up.

Maschio's henchmen watched Conrad

closely to ensure that he did not regurgitate the substance. Conrad's choking subsided. He lifted his head and grinned at them both.

"Alright. Let's go," he boomed enthusiastically.

7

Maschio's henchmen blindfolded Jerry and Conrad, unbound Conrad's legs, led them both to a car, and then, drove them far away from Maschio's hide out. In accordance with Maschio's wishes, Jerry and Conrad laid down on the floor of the back seat of the car so that no one would see them.

A perky song with a lot of electronic noises in it was playing on the radio.

"Disco, disco, dude! Shake that booty,

shake that booty! Disco dude! You are the disco dude! Yeah—" Fernando sang along with the radio. He sang many of the lyrics wrong and his voice was very shrill and off-key.

"That's *it*! Enough! Enough of this shit!" Lorenzo yelled after awhile. "You are *not allowed* to touch the radio anymore!"

Lorenzo turned the dial on the radio, changing the station.

"Paaainnn!" the man on the radio shrieked to the sound of squealing electric guitars. "Aaaanggsst! Fuck society! Fuck rules! My dads don't understand me!   I an't got time for school! So fuck you—" An intense electric guitar solo played, while the singer screamed into his microphone.

An hour passed. Lorenzo's death metal rang in Jerry's ears. The car moved quickly, taking a turn or weaving between other cars every so often. After some time, the car stopped. Jerry heard a couple of car doors slam as Lorenzo and Fernando emerged.

Lorenzo climbed into the back of the car, pulled a switch blade out of the pocket of his jeans, and cut the ropes that bound Conrad's wrists. Then, he removed Conrad's blindfold. Fernando opened the other door and removed Jerry's blind fold as well.

"Get out," Lorenzo instructed.

Jerry and Conrad stood up and stumbled out of the car on to the sand. They had been driven to a deserted place at the very edge of

Manazonia, where the city of Mantropolis ended and The Strange Lands began. The grey skyscrapers and stone townhouses here had once been a part of the living city, but now, it seemed, the Strange Lands beasts had reduced the structures to ghosts; burned them black, crushed them to rubble and, in some places, twisted them off of their steel foundations. This was a quiet, deserted place, where cracked cement streets tapered off slowly and gave way to yellow sand. An ominous wind whistled through the air and blew tumble weeds and grains of sand around Jerry and Conrad's feet.

"Huh..." Jerry murmured as he observed his strange surroundings. He had never been so close to the edge of Manazonia before. There were boarders and fences restricting access to ordinary citizens and Jerry had not been working in the field as an agent for the Company very long.

Lorenzo and Fernando jumped back in the car. Jerry heard the sound of them snapping the doors shut and driving away into the distance but he did not watch them leave. Instead, he stared at one burnt and twisted building. The hot afternoon sun gleamed against its sharp broken windows and scrunched, exposed support beams.

"What happened here?" Jerry inquired of Conrad, sounding far away.

"What, this?" Conrad said, shrugging. "This has been here forever. It's no big thing."

"Right. So *what* happened here?"

"Strange Lands beasts," explained Conrad. He began to walk forward, winding his way around piles of twisted support beams and debris. Jerry followed.

"Strange Lands beasts did this?"

"Yea, some of them are huge. All of them are destructive." said Conrad. "Some breathe fire. Others squirt acid or crush boulders like they're made of Styrofoam."

Conrad and Jerry walked past a couple of smoldering craters in the cement, a statue of a naked man holding a flute with its head knocked off, and a few piles of broken wood and gravel, twice as high as Conrad was tall.

"Like...that giant Cyclops thing that got

into the city?" Jerry asked.

"Yea, like that," Conrad said, he wasn't looking at Jerry when he spoke to him but rather observing his surroundings cautiously, large hands balled into fists, muscles tense.

"I read about that in the paper," said Jerry. "You were the one that killed it, weren't you?"

"Yea," responded Conrad as he kicked through some rubble and chunks of broken cement. "The city is back this way," said Conrad, pointing into the distance. "Maschio's men must have let us go here so that no one would notice them remove our restraints and blindfolds."

"Yea, that would have been suspicious," agreed Jerry. As he followed Conrad through the dead, broken city, its structures became gradually less burned, broken, and otherwise damaged. "So...you're the man that they say...slaughters Strange Lands beasts better than any other man?"

"I guess," said Conrad. "I have taken out a few of them before. That's probably why they sent me after Lucy. But yea, I'm not as good at it as they say."

"No?"

"The thing with the eye, the news named it Death Eye," said Conrad.

"Yea, I remember that. Pht...*Death Eye*. Stupid," said Jerry.

"It killed my last partner," said Conrad. "Stuffed him in its mouth and swallowed him whole."

"Oh," said Jerry. "I'm sorry, Conrad. Was he your friend?"

"An ex-boyfriend actually," said Conrad. "His name was Wyatt Parker."

"Oh. What was he like?"

"Eh...our relationship was never really more than physical while it lasted, which wasn't long."

"Oh, *really*," Jerry replied with a grin and a cocked eyebrow, "Because *I heard* you proposed to him. Is that true?"

Conrad stared pensively into the distance for a moment, and recalled his old partner, Wyatt Parker, for a moment. The man had been tall and slender with a large Addam's apple and an uncommonly deep voice.

"I was drunk...," Conrad admitted after some time had passed, "And maybe I let myself get too attached...but I knew it was a mistake as soon as I did it. Wyatt was the independent type. He was the kind of guy who always did what he wanted to and didn't give a crap about what anybody thought of it. He had a lot of confidence and he always spoke his mind bluntly, even when what he had to say was cruel. Maybe even *especially* when it was cruel...So, basically, you know, he was a loudmouthed little turd...but he was still my partner and it was my job to make sure he made it home alive. I didn't, so that makes me not as great at slaying the Strange Lands beasts as everyone says."

"Don't blame yourself, Conrad. I'm sure it's not your fault," said Jerry, though he could not be sure if this was true. Conrad could be so cocky and irresponsible. Wyatt's death *might* have been Conrad's fault.

"I don't," said Conrad. "It's just weird to watch people die, you know? It's not all clean and nice like in the movies."

"Yea, you don't have to tell me that," laughed Jerry, remembering the shredded brain meat of the dead stripper and the grotesque way that it had dangled from the man's open skull cavity.

The two men reached a large, steel wall that seemed to stretch endlessly upward into the sky.

———

"This is the edge of the barrier," Conrad explained.   "Manazonia is contained within a large border fence to protect it from being destroyed by Strange Lands beasts.   The entrance to the city must be a little further East. C'mon let's go."

After ten minutes or so of walking, Conrad and Jerry reached the entrance to the barrier. There was a metal door here with a slot built into the side of it.   Conrad inserted his Company ID into the slot and the metal door slid upward, revealing the tall buildings, and busy crowded streets of Mantropolis within.

8

The   Birthing   Factory   was   a   large, rectangular, windowless building, made of dull grey metal and surrounded by a steel mesh fence topped with barbed wire. Black-uniformed guards with flat topped hats and long rifles stood at all of the building's entrances. These men were still, like statues; expressions blank; feet set apart; gripping weapons with both hands.

Conrad and Jerry approached the building's front entrance, which was an archway in the mesh fence. A pair of black uniformed guards stood on either side of it.

"What's your business here," one of the guards inquired of Conrad and Jerry as they reached the entrance.

"We're Company Men on official business," Conrad informed the guard, flashing his ID.

"Right. We have an official policy for this," said the guard. "All visitors need an escort when they tour the birthing factory, even agents from The Company. Hold on, let me call you a guide."

The guard took a black, two-way radio off of his belt and pushed a few buttons on it. Then, lifted it up to his mouth.

"Yea, Jeff," said the guard to the man on the other end of the two way radio. "We've got a couple of Company Men here on official business.....Yea, uhhuh...They want to tour the factory."

The guard put the two way radio back on his belt.

"Jeff'll be here in a minute," said the guard to Conrad and Jerry. "He'll be your guide through the factory during your investigation.

A few minutes passed. A chubby, middle-aged man with thick glasses and a powder blue bow tie emerged from the factory. He wore a grey suit jacket and slacks, and his brown hair was parted directly down the middle.

"Welcome, friends," the funny looking little man greeted them warmly. He had a hint of a southern accent and a frozen smile that never flickered. "My name is Jeff and I will be your guide this evening."

"Hello Jeff," Jerry and Conrad murmured in unison.

"Well, golly, this is exciting," said Jeff with the jovial tone of an experienced tour guide. "I've been a guide here for 10 years but I've never escorted a Company Man before!"

Jeff turned and walked toward the entrance of the factory. Conrad and Jerry followed.

"Welcome to the birthing factory," Jeff said, opening the front door of the factory wide. Conrad and Jerry walked through it and into a large, high-ceiling-ed metal room, the floor of which was lined with metal boxes. The shrieking of thousands of infants filled the air.

"This is the nursery room," explained Jeff, gesturing toward the little metal boxes with his arms. "Home to thousands of nature's little miracles!"

Jerry peered down into one of the boxes and saw a tiny wriggling baby in a powder blue onesy, laying on top of a folded white blanket, and sucking a powder blue pacifier. It had large, blue eyes and a chubby pink face.

"After nine months of growing big and strong inside of their own individual, surrogate incubators, these darling children are ready and waiting to be delivered to their loving fathers!" said Jeff, sounding very rehearsed. His frozen grin was becoming rather obnoxious.

A few men in powder blue jumpsuits and caps, circled the room. Every so often they would stop in front of a metal box, lift the infant out of it and change its diaper or feed it a bottle.

Jeff pointed to one of the men in the powder blue uniforms.

"And these fellas take care of the infants until each one is ready to be delivered to his forever home, via the birthing truck! But don't worry, none of these darling children will go very long without a home! Each one was ordered nine months ago by a pair of doting fathers, with clear criminal records, who have filled out copious paper work, and undergone extensive psychological testing! Only the most moral and upstanding men will be approved as suitable parents by The Company!"

Jeff paused as though expecting the two men to celebrate this.

"...Yay....," cheered Jerry uncertainly when

it seemed that Jeff would not continue his tour without some affirmation of this statement. He now understood why Maschio wanted that surrogate incubator so badly. A man with his criminal record would never have been approved for fatherhood by The Company. Perhaps he wanted to keep his drug enterprise in the family.

Jeff walked for awhile through the factory, Jerry and Conrad followed him, silently. Jeff led Jerry and Conrad into another room, and then, kept walking until he came to a dull metal wall covered in gleaming steel doors. A few metal tubes slides were built into the top of the wall and every so often an infant would slide out of the bottom off one. These babies were not clean and pretty like the ones in the metal boxes, however. They were shrieking and covered in frothy bloody discharge. A grotesque tube protruded from each of their belly buttons.

"What the—," Conrad gasped in confusion.

"Gross...I think I'm going to be sick," said Jerry, covering his mouth with both of his hands.

"This is the beauty of nature, boys!" announced Jeff cheerfully. "We were all born naked and bloody! But with any luck we won't die that way...ah haha! I'm joking! I'm a jokester!"

"...Funny," said Jerry, and then, he forced a rather unconvincing fake laugh.

The bloody babies were caught by men in

blue uniforms, their gross cords were removed with sharp scissors. Then, the babies were washed clean in tiny metal sinks built into the floor. The men then passed the babies to the next man on their respective assembly line. The second man in each line put the babies down on a table, diapered them, dressed them in a powder blue onesy and stuck a powder blue pacifier in their mouths. They then put the babies on a conveyer belt and they were carried away to the next room.

"That conveyer belt leads to the nursery room." said Jeff.

"But where do those tubes lead?" Jerry asked.

"To the surrogate incubator rooms," said

Jeff quickly, waving a hand dismissively. "This concludes our tour of the human birthing factory! Next, let's see where animals are born!"

"Yea, we didn't come here to see the livestock," said Conrad. "We've come to investigate those surrogate incubators."

"Oh no, sir. You can't see the surrogate incubators. No one can," said Jeff. "I've never even seen them."

"We're on official company business. Now *show us* the surrogate incubators," growled Conrad menacingly.

"I can do that, sir. I'm under strict orders not to let anyone in there without extensive screening and paper work," said Jeff. "If you'd like to come back later, the whole process should take about five days. You should get a call from the factory when your paper work's been approved, your Company affiliations have been confirmed, and your temporary identification pass cards have been printed."

"Is there anyway we could speed that process up? Just a bit?" Jerry asked cautiously.

"No," replied Jeff bluntly. "Five days is a conservative estimate, sir. It usually takes more like two weeks."

"What about if we gave you a bribe? Do you take bribes?" Jerry asked innocently.

"No," replied Jeff bluntly.

Jerry took a fifty dollar bill out of his pocket.

"Here, have a fifty," he said, shoving the

bill in Jeff's direction.

"Gee, thanks," said Jeff, and he shoved the bill into his pocket.

Jerry looked at Jeff expectantly. Jeff stared back, the frozen smile had melted from his lips now.

"You still can't go in," said Jeff. He did not hand the fifty that Jerry had given him back, but rather, kept it in his pocket. "Fill out the paperwork, then wait for the factory to call."

"Fuck, man! We an't got that kind'a time!" Conrad swore in exasperation.

"Sir, there are children here," said Jeff, sounding appalled.

"They're newborns," groaned Conrad. "They don't even understand English yet!"

He picked one of the clean, dressed infants off of a nearby conveyor belt and started talking to it in a baby voice: "Fuck, fuck, fuck, fuck, shit, fucker, balls."

The baby wiggled in his hands and looked up at him stupidly. He put it back down on the conveyor belt and it was pulled away into the next room.

"Sir, you can comport yourself in an appropriate manner or leave," said Jeff.

"How about this," said Conrad. He pulled a gun out from under his shirt and aimed it at Jeff's head. "You can cooperate with The Company or die."

Every factory worker in the room had their eyes on Conrad now.

"Conrad, stop!" Jerry shouted. "He's just doing his job!"

"And I'm doing mine," growled Conrad. "I am authorized to kill anyone who interferes with official company business and he's pissing me off."

"Conrad, there has to be a better way."

"Fine," said Conrad, lowering his gun. "My fathers are Luis and Rodman Ryder, co-Executive Heads of The Company and the only men alive who have spoken directly with The Overlords. Cooperate or they will kill you."

"Fine, fine. Whatever," said Jeff. Then, he dug a key out of the pocket of his slacks and shoved it in Conrad's direction. "Here's the key. Just don't kill me. Also, don't touch anything while you're in there."

Conrad ripped the key out of Jeff's hand and started walking toward one of the metal doors in the wall underneath of the silver tube slides. A laminated paper sign with the words "employees only" was stuck there under a frame of clear tape.

"See," Conrad bragged, wiggling his eyebrows at Jerry. "Now, who's good at *negotiating*?"

Jeff watched as Conrad and Jerry unlocked the door, walked inside, and slammed it shut behind them. Then, he took a black two-way radio off of his belt. It had been concealed under his suit jacket.

"Yea, Eddy," he said, holding the two way

radio up to his mouth. "We've got some trouble makers in the S I room. Send in some armed guards."

9

The surrogate incubator room was very dark. Conrad stumbled around a bit, feeling for a light switch but, instead, he felt a cold metal wall a few feet to his left, and a cold metal railing a few feet to his right. He kicked something with his foot that was probably Jerry.

"*Ow!* God damn it, Conrad! Are you trying to break my legs!"

"How was I supposed to know you were there?"

Jerry and Conrad resumed flailing around in the dark, searching for a light switch.

Then, Jerry answered: "You need to be more caref-aaagghhhhhhhh!"

Conrad accidentally walked into Jerry again, knocking him down. Jerry screamed and as he screamed his voice seemed to be getting farther and farther way. A lot of loud banging noises that might have been Jerry's head and body clunking against something metal accompanied the screaming.

"Jerry?" Conrad asked, sounding confused. His eyes were beginning to adjust to the darkness a bit but he still couldn't see where Jerry had fallen.

The lights flickered on. Conrad blinked. This was a large, tall metal room, with lines of fluorescent lighting built into the ceiling.

Conrad looked down and noticed that he was standing on an elevated metal pathway along the edge of the room. There was a dull metal wall to his left and an mesh railing to his right.

Conrad took a few steps forward and glanced down at the steep austere stairway. Jerry lay on the floor at the bottom of it; the back of his head and shoulders, resting against a large, metal lever, built into the floor. There was a glazed look in his eye.

"...Jerry?" Conrad murmured.

"I'm fine," said Jerry quickly. He stood up and started limping toward the top of the next stairway, which was at the end of a second narrow platform. "Seriously."

Conrad wandered to the edge of the

platform, put his hand on the top of the railing, and stared straight down.

"Uh....*Jerry?*" Conrad muttered darkly.

"What?" Jerry asked, limping over to where Conrad was standing.

Conrad leaned over the railing, his mouth a gape. He lifted a large hand and pointed downward.

Jerry reached the edge of the platform. Gripped the railing with both bony hands, and stared down.

"Jesus, Joseph, and Manny, that's grim," Jerry swore quietly, his mouth falling open with his disillusionment.

Below the railing where Jerry and Conrad stood, were hundreds upon hundreds of clear glass tubes, stacked into pillars, one on top of another. The pillars were organized into neat rows, and each pillar was covered in an assortment of tubes and wires, some clear, some opaque grey. At points the tubes converged with each other and became one larger tube, ending in the floor, the walls, or the ceiling.

Conrad Jogged down the remaining steps to get a better look at what was inside of the tubes. Jerry limped slowly behind him.

There was no mistaking it now, each tube contained the headless, limbless torso of a shman, suspended in fluid. A bundle of grey tubes protruded from the empty neck hole of each shman. Conrad walked up to one, curiously. Its skin was very pail and a pair of clear tubes protruded from each of its nipples. Periodically, a burst of white fluid would be sucked through those tubes and into the floor. Conrad looked down, past a plump stomach that stuck out like a beach ball and a pair of stitched-up scars where the thing's legs had presumably once been. It looked as though they had been removed vertically from the hips. A clear tube the size of a human infant protruded from beneath the shman's body. Conrad glanced around. Every now and then a bloody infant trailing a gross chord was sucked out of one of the shmen through a clear, fluid-filled tube and into one of the walls, presumably to be washed, dressed, and delivered to their homes, via the birthing truck.

"Hey, Jerry?...*Jerry?*" Conrad called. He glanced around in search of the other man, who was being bizarrely quiet.

Conrad spotted the back of Jerry's auburn head and blue suit jacket a few dozen feet or so in the distance and walked over to him. Jerry seemed to be entranced by one shman, suspended in a fluid-filled tube, directly in front of him. This one was smaller than some of the others and ghostly pail. The growths on its chest were small almost to the point of being nonexistent.

"Jerry?" Conrad called again.

Jerry was silent and did not respond. He did not turn his head to look at Conrad.

"....Jerry?"

"This is a *child*, Conrad," murmured Jerry quietly, again, not turning to look at him.

"What? How can you tell?" Conrad asked.

"It's younger than the other ones. I've just got this feeling," said Jerry.

"Well if we're going to take one to Maschio. It might be easier to grab a smaller, lighter one," said Conrad.

"These tubes are probably keeping it alive. If we remove it from the jar, it'll be dead before we can leave here with it," said Jerry.

"Hey, you!" A deep, caustic voice accused.

Conrad turned in the direction of the voice. A wiry, forty-something man with a large bald spot and a bushy brown mustache ambled over to them. He was wearing a dark blue jumpsuit and was holding a mop in one hand and a tool box in the other.

"Yea, you!" the man said. "No one's allowed in here except for the maintenance men!"

"We're maintenance men," said Jerry quietly, without turning around. "In training."

"Oh, well why didn't you just say so!" said the man, sounding entirely more friendly. He grinned. "My name is Earl, and welcome to the surrogate incubator room."

Jerry turned around, stone faced.

"It's good to be here," Jerry said quietly.

Conrad nodded in agreement. Earl stared

at Conrad for a moment.

"You're buddy's a looker," Earl said to Jerry, pointing the brush end of his mop toward Conrad. "He's got sort of a famous face. Feel like I've seen it somewhere before."

"Nah. Everybody says that," said Conrad. He put his hand out for the maintenance man to shake. "The name's Stew."

Earl stuck the tool box he was holding in the crook of his elbow and shook Conrad's hand.

"Stew," Earl repeated. "Welcome."

He turned toward Jerry.

"...And you are?"

"Edd," lied Jerry quickly.

"...Well, since you guys're new. I suppose it's only fair that I give you the tour," said Earl.

"Follow me, you guys. I'll show you around."

Earl started walking between two rows of stacked surrogate incubators. Jerry and Conrad followed.

"While you're here, your job will be to check these tubes for leaks and damage," said Earl. He stopped walking, knelt down, and opened his tool box, then, removed a wad of grey putty. "When you see a leak in the tubing, patch it up with some of this adhesive putty. Then, file an incident report so that the birthing factory can send a technician to make a more permanent repair."

Earl put the putty back in his tool box, then, snapped it shut. He stood up and removed a notepad from the breast pocket of his dark blue jump suit.

"Keep something to write with on your person at all times. And then if you see damage to the tubes, write down the number of the surrogate incubator closest to the damage. If the damage is to a tube linking two surrogate incubators, write down the number of the two surrogate incubators the damage is between."

"Excuse me," Jerry interrupted. "Where are the numbers?"

Earl returned the notepad to his breast pocket.

"The tubes are labeled on top," Earl said. He pointed to an oval metal tag built into the flat metal top of a nearby cylinder. The cylinder held a tall, dark-skinned shman. The number

5128 was engraved there in a bold, gothic font.

"So say," Earl picked up a tube running out of the 5128 cylinder and shook it in his hand. "There's a rip in this here tube. You just stick the putty on the rip, write down the number 5128, and file an incident report at the end of your shift."

"Alright then," said Conrad.

"Alright guys, come with me," Earl said and he began to move again. Jerry and Conrad followed. "The other part of your job is that you've got to clean up the mess when the lines break. Recently we had a mishap with the feces line running off of the origin room. The pipes have been repaired...but man...is there a mess! I'm talkin' piles of shit as far as the eye can see!"

"Yea, sorry I'm allergic to cleaning piles of shit," said Conrad only half jokingly. "That sounds like a job for my buddy-"

"Edd," Jerry reminded, in case Conrad was about to forget and use Jerry's real name.

"Edd," Conrad finished. "He loves cleaning piles of shit. You should definitely let him do it."

"Gee thanks, *Stew*, thanks for looking out for me," said Jerry sarcastically.

Earl walked for awhile. The place was pretty large and without the old maintenance man as a guide, it might have been pretty easy to get lost. The rows of surrogate incubators all looked more or less alike. As they walked, however, Jerry watched the numbers on the rows of tubes with careful diligence. They seemed to be getting lower with every passing second. Jerry counted them off silently in his mind,....*four thousand....three thousand....two thousand....*

"Say, Earl," Jerry piped up as he noticed the two thousands engraved on the surrogate incubators were now *one* thousands. "How is this place set up anyway?"

"What do you mean?"

"I mean....the numbers...is there any rhyme or reason to them?"

"Actually yes...I think they're kind of *like*....in a circle or something? You can find any incubator if you have its number but it's a little bit tricky...I think you have to go up and down the rows or something like that. I've been told that the whole thing is just like a big circle. You'll get used to it. But it can be a little bit confusing at first," said Earl.

"Did you hear that, Stew?" Jerry said to Conrad. Earl had his back to them so Jerry winked twice to get his point a cross. "It's like *a circle.*"

"Right. And you care...*because*?" Conrad replied stupidly.

"Circles begin where they end," Jerry finished dramatically, raising his eyebrows.

"Oh....I get it," Conrad said, remembering Lucy's riddle.

The engravings above the cylinders were in the 500's now and Jerry was beginning to notice something about the surrogate incubators: in general, they got smaller (and *younger*?) as their numbers went down. Their leg-less hips got narrower. The growths on their chests got flatter, and then, nonexistent.

Conrad must have noticed this too because he asked: "So what's up with the number system? Do you arrange them by size?"

"No," said Earl. "What happens is, when expired incubators are terminated, younger incubators are moved to a space with a higher number to make room for fresh incubators in The Origin Room."

They were in the 200's now. Here the tubes were smaller and the shmen were as small as toddlers.

"And this is all on the down low, huh?" asked Conrad. "How do you even keep a secret like this?"

"Oh, I have to," said Earl. "And you should too. If you tell anyone you're not supposed to, The Birthing Factory will send Company men to execute you for treason."

"But I heard that Company men aren't allowed in here," said Jerry.

"Oh, they're not," said Earl. "But the second you stepped foot outside of this place, those monsters would be on you like flies. Not that you'd make it that far. There's a special squad of highly skilled assassins, called The Excution Squad, who act as security here. They are our first line of defense against thieves and spies."

The three men walked until they reached a tall, metal wall with a small metal door in it. Earl removed a key from his pocket, unlocked the door, and then, walked through it. Jerry and Conrad followed.

The shrieking of infants and rapid whirling of machine parts hit them all, like a fist to both eardrums. In this room, the cylinders were only as large as fish tanks and they contained the trunks of headless, limbless, infants. All tubes were present in miniature, except for the largest, birthing tube, and the two nipple tubes, witch, it seemed, had not yet been installed. The torsos here were more complete than the older ones. They still had their genitalia and all of their pelvises, where as in older shmen, it seemed, that these things had been removed to make room for the birthing tubes.

A colorful infant's mural splattered some areas of the wall in this room. It featured a smiling sun and moon, radiating with yellow and blue lines, an anthropomorphic fox, holding a pair of binoculars and riding a hot air balloon, and a row of smiling daisies with faces. They assaulted Jerry with their ironic cheerfulness. Was this mural someone's idea of a joke?

Conrad seemed unconcerned by the mural and unconcerned by the whole surrogate incubator room in general. He seemed more curious than anything else and had many questions for Earl, the maintenance man.

"So these are baby shmen?" Conrad asked Earl.

"Yup," confirmed Earl.

"Do you think they're in pain?" Conrad asked. He sounded more curious than concerned.

"Not a chance," said Earl. "All shmen are born paralyzed and with empty brain cavities, so their unnecessary appendages are circumcised at birth to save space and stasis fluid throughout its lifetime."

"Wow. Cool," said Conrad.

The shrieking of infants and the whirling of what must have been blades in the next room cut through the air.

"So why are they screaming like that?"

Conrad asked curiously.

"It's just a reflex," explained Earl. "Shmen don't feel things the way baby boys do."

"Neat," said Conrad, grinning.

The three men kept walking. Jerry put his hands in his pockets and stayed very silent.

"So what's in the next room," Conrad asked.

The smell of fresh human waste was growing as they walked and Conrad realized that they must have been approaching the mess left by the broken fecal tube.

"There's a sorting machine in the next room," explained Earl. "Male and shmale infants are identified and separated there."

"Wow...cool...Can we see that next?"

Conrad asked excitedly.

"Can we *not* see that next *please*?" Jerry chimed in. He lifted his white, button down shirt over his mouth and nose to block out the stench of the approaching pile of feces.

.   Conrad glanced down at his watch. Time was slipping by. Maschio's deadline was fast approaching. And the neurotoxin was surely rushing through his veins, ready to render him (and Jerry) as immobile and catatonic as shmen. Jerry too was aware of the passage of time and he glanced at the headless infants in tubes as he walked by them, wondering how they might be connected to the floor of the room and if it were possible to grab one and run with it.

As they walked, a large pile of rank feces

that seemed as large and as tall as two mac trucks stacked on top of each other, appeared in the distance. As they approached it slowly came into sharper focus. It must have covered rows of the infant incubators because their tubes emerged from the shit pile on every side.

"Christ, I hate this job," said Earl.

"You know what, man," said Conrad, clapping Earl on the back. "Don't even worry about it."

"Huh? How am I supposed to not worry about it? It's a giant pile of shit. I'm the maintenance man," said Earl, motioning toward himself.

"Hey, man. Just leave your mop and cleaning stuff here and *we* will *take care of it.*

Take a break, man. Go out for lunch or something. We got this," said Conrad.

"Wow, thanks man," said Earl. "You sure?"

"Sure, I'm sure," said Conrad cheerfully. "Now get outta' here. Go, *go!*"

"Life is too short," said Jerry grimly. "God knows you've suffered enough."

"Alright, well thanks, you guys," said Earl and he turned to leave. "I really appreciate this."

Jerry and Conrad watched him as he disappeared into the distance and after he was finally gone, the door to The Origin Room having snapped shut behind him, Conrad turned toward Jerry and said: "Alright, he's gone. Now let's grab one of these things and get the hell out of here."

Conrad knelt down and grabbed one of the cylinders on the floor with both hands.

"Conrad, wait!" Jerry said quickly.

Conrad let go of the cylinder and looked up at him.

"I think we should take number 9999," Jerry finished. "She might be a clue."

10

Jerry and Conrad ran past rows of incubators to the 100's, then 50's and finally the 10's. There was the cylinder marked 9999, right next to the cylinder marked 0001.

"This is it," whispered Jerry morosely. "The beginning and the end. Her number is 9999…just like Lucy's riddle said."

Conrad knelt down, grabbed incubator 9999 with both hands and pulled. It would not be moved.

"It's bolted to the floor," Conrad grunted as he attempted to lift the thing once more.

Jerry knelt down and looked at the metal part of the cylinder, which connected it to the surrounding floor.

"They must have put it in here somehow," Jerry said, and then, he noticed a groove in the cylinder's metal base. "Try turning it."

Conrad twisted the metal cylinder right but it did not move.

"Try the other way," Jerry insisted.

Conrad twisted the cylinder left and this time it did move. He kept turning it, until the thing was unscrewed from the floor. It was still connected by its many tubes however.

"What do we do about the tubes?" Conrad asked. He glanced down at his watch again, getting nervous.

"Well...um...," Jerry fumbled, glancing nervously down at his own wrist watch. "I guess...."

"Do you think it'll die without the tubes?"

"Um....," Jerry contemplated nervously. "Maybe. But that isn't our concern. It just has to live long enough for Maschio to give us the antidote."

Conrad took a long, sharp knife off of a loop on his belt.

"So cut the tubes, then?" Conrad asked.

"Cut the tubes," Jerry confirmed grimly and he nodded.

Conrad began sawing through the pair of large grey tubes protruding from the incubator's neck and through the top of the cylinder. The first one bled clear water when it was cut and gushed it when it was severed. The second one spurted an opaque white liquid, which sprayed Conrad's face and clothes.

"What the fuck is that?" Jerry swore. The fact that he did not know what the liquid was made it much more gross.

Conrad licked some of it off of his lips and Jerry cringed.

"Relax it's just milk," he said. Then, he began sawing the two tubes protruding from the bottom of the cylinder, which anchored the thing to the floor. These tubes squirted urine and feces and a nasty smelling mixture of the two vile substances gathered in a pool at their feet.

An alarm began to whirl at ear-shredding volume. A few red lights built into the ceiling flashed on and off, periodically bathing the metal room in an eerie blood red light.

Conrad grabbed Jerry by the arm and started pulling him along as he ran. His other arm hugged headless, floating infant number 9999 to his chest. Its jagged tubes flew behind him, spraying drops of water, milk, urine, and feces as he ran.

11

Conrad ran, his left hand tight around

Jerry's forearm, his right arm cradling the dripping, headless infant.   Black-uniformed execution squad men, holding long, black rifles emerged from a row of metal doors and past a chaotic pastel-colored mural of an anthropomorphic dish and spoon dancing under the moon.   Here also, a bull with a huge, shit-eating grin was pictured jumping over the moon.

Black-clad Execution Squad men organized themselves into tight rows, aimed their rifles and started shooting as they ran. Conrad started running in zig-zags to avoid the racing bullets but the weight of Jerry's small body was starting to slow him down.   Half limping, half jogging on legs damaged from his fall down the flight of steps, the shorter man was basically dead weight being dragged.

A sharp pain shot through Conrad's shoulder as a pair of bullets were imbedded in his flesh. His hand loosened and slipped off of Jerry's arm. Then, Jerry stumbled and fell.

Conrad turned, pulled a pair of guns from the loops on his belt, and opened fire on The Execution Squad. He shot a man in the neck and the man fell. His hands flew to his gushing neck and crimson blood spilled over his large, sausage-like fingers. Then, he collapsed.

"You son-of-a-bastard!" one of the remaining men screamed. He shot at Conrad a few times and Conrad darted out of the way. He cringed as the final bullet grazed the edge of his left ear, then, grabbed the gun out of the approaching executioner's hand, flipped it around, and shot him in the face with it. The man's face was blown from his skull and he collapsed at Conrad's feet.

The executioners must have been running out of bullets because now half of them were stopping to reload and the other half were between their reloading comrades and the enemy. They ran at Conrad and Jerry with their empty rifles raised, ready to swing them like clubs.

Jerry sat up, pulled his gun from a loop on his belt, and unloaded its contents in the chest of a man who was running toward him with his rifle raised high, ready to smash Jerry's head in with it. The man coughed up blood and collapsed in a pile next to where Jerry was sitting. Jerry staggered to his feet and began limping forward, his gun raised.

A second man, wielding an empty gun like a bludgeon ran towards him and Jerry shot this man square in the center of his forehead. The man's legs crumbled underneath of him and he fell down dead. Jerry clicked his gun again but this time nothing happened. It was empty.

A third man ran toward Jerry and knocked him backward, bludgeoning him in the face with the handle of his rifle. Jerry lurched forward and spat blood and teeth onto the ground. The man raised his gun high, intent on clocking Jerry over the head with it. Then,

Conrad ran toward this man, brought back his large fist and clocked him in the face with it. The man was knocked backward, his hand loosening on the barrel of his empty rifle. Conrad swooped down, threw Jerry over his shoulder, and started running with him.

The Execution Squad was shooting again. Conrad kept running, weaving between stacks of infant incubators to avoid the barrage of bullets. There was a loud smashing sound that must have been cylinders being cracked by stray shots. Liquid poured from the cracks in the cylinders and the infant torsos sank lower, their tubes coiling beneath them. This gave Conrad an idea.

Conrad ran through the door that linked

the origin room to the rest of the surrogate incubator rooms. The Execution squad followed, led by their massive captain, they spilled through the door, which linked The Origin room to surrounding rooms.

Jerry threw his empty gun at the captain and it hit him in the forehead, cracking his skull. Blood squirted from his head and he crumbled to the floor. A couple of Execution Squad men tripped over his massive body. And in the second that they were distracted, Conrad shot his last remaining bullet and hit a tank in the ceiling. Festering fecal matter exploded from the tank and gathered in piles all around them. It was piling up like a mountain, covering the fallen Execution Squad men as they struggled to get up.

Conrad fumbled, struggling to hold on to the headless infant, Jerry, and his gun. Then, he dropped the gun and kept running.

<u>12</u>

The world was a disorienting rush of ear-stabbing sirens and shooting splotches of color. A churning, nauseous pain came over Conrad but he didn't have time to wonder if this was the result of the blood loss from the bullet wounds in his shoulder or the early effects of Maschio's neurotoxin. Probably it was some combination of both.

Conrad ran past a pair of confused security guards and back to the parking lot. His vision was beginning to fade and he stumbled as the world shook all around him, struggling to right itself.

"Hey! You can't um...you can't leave!" one of the security guards called unsurely. He was busy spreading cream cheese on a toasted bagel and seemed unsure about whether or not he was going to bother with running after Conrad.

Conrad ran to his car and jumped over the side of the driver's side door, just as his vision faded to white, his limbs began to convulse wildly, and thick frothy foam poured from his gasping mouth.

"Conrad? *Conrad!*" Jerry called out, pulling himself away from the convulsing man's loose grip. Conrad's other hand opened and the surrogate incubator rolled onto the floor in front of the driver's side seat. A flash of something white, taped to the underside of the incubator's cylinder, caught Jerry's eye. This must have been Lucy's clue.

"They uh…they went that way," said one of the guards through a mouth full of toasted bagel. And, as he said this, he pointed four or five shit-caked Execution Squad men in the direction of the parking lot.

"Fuck," Jerry swore.

The Execution Squad men were running toward the car, guns raised. Conrad was twitching and frothing at the mouth, his large, muscular limbs convulsing wildly. Jerry grabbed Conrad's car keys out of the back pocket of his loose jeans and rammed them into the ignition of the car. Speeding off, out of the parking lot, and onto the street, just as the execution squad men began firing.

Jerry sped down the road toward the corner of Arrow and Fifth Street, the location where he had agreed to meet Maschio's men and exchange the surrogate incubator for the antidote. He glanced in the rearview mirror. Two black armored cars were speeding down the road, weaving between traffic with well practiced skill and precision.

"Fuck," Jerry swore and he put his foot down on the gas, racing forward past a gas station, a Lardo's Lard Shack, an x-rated video store, and a sports supplies store, then, taking a sharp turn, onto Cooper Street. Jerry glanced at the rearview mirror. The armored cars were getting closer. Their blacked out windows rolled down and the heads and shoulder's of rifle wielding execution squad men emerged. A pair of men emerged from both sun roofs of the two armored cars, wielding massive, silver machine guns.

"Fuck," Jerry swore again and he sped forward, dipping between speeding cars and racing through stop signs and red traffic lights. During training, Company Men were taught to drive this way in case an emergency situation occurred, which required a quick get away or a swift capture of a wanted man. So, Jerry had done this kind of thing before, and also, as a

Company Man, had the privilege to break traffic laws basically any time he wanted to for basically any reason. He just didn't abuse the privilege the way that Conrad did.

The Execution Squad men continued firing off rounds. Jerry sped forward and took another sharp turn to avoid the barrage of bullets. He glanced quickly down at Conrad who was still splayed across Jerry's legs. His body twitched and a frothy, white liquid poured from his open mouth, dampening the fabric of Jerry's pants and the crimson upholstery. The noise of six or seven bullets hitting the back of the car filled Jerry's ears and he snapped back to attention, accelerating as he took another sharp turn.

Jerry glanced back up at the rear view mirror. The two black armored cars were closing in on either side of him as he raced down the road. Bullets were flying at Conrad's car from either side. Jerry ducked to avoid them and, in a leap of faith, slammed his foot down on the gas to shoot forward blindly. Perhaps his pursuers were attempting to collision execute (a phrase from the Car Chase 101 text book that Jerry had memorized in college. It meant "to terminate a criminal by way of intentional car accident.").

There was a loud noise, the smashing of metal against metal, the frustrated screams of many deep-voiced men. Jerry popped his head back up and glanced at the review mirror. Two black armored cars smashed into each other and toppled onto their sides. It seemed, Jerry's hunch about his pursuers' plan to collision execute had been correct. The two armored cars had converged on his car, but missed smashing it into an accordion and, instead, crashed into each other.

Jerry raced forward, and turned left on to 5th Street. In the distance, he saw the hotel on the corner, where 5th Street converged with Arrow Street. There was a black limousine there. Jerry slammed his foot on the break, grabbed the infant incubator, jumped over the driver's side door, and sprinted toward the limousine.

As he was running, Jerry felt Lucy's clue

(a folded piece of paper taped to the underside of the tube) with his hand, ripped the paper off, and shoved it into the pocket of his slacks. The blacked-out driver's side window of the Limousine rolled down slowly and a man with gelled-back black hair and a purple-studded nose ring stared out at Jerry. He adjusted his sunglasses coolly and frowned, refusing to allow Jerry's apparent distress to rile him.

"I...I've got the surrogate incubator," Jerry panted. His heart was racing. He gasped for air, and glanced behind him to see if the Execution Squad men were still in pursuit. He saw nothing but the flickering neon sign of a cheap hotel silhouetted against the darkening sky.

"Please. Hurry. We...we need the antidote. Conrad hasn't got much time," Jerry stuttered his heart racing, his breathing heavy.

"Hm...yes...," said Maschio's henchman slowly and indifferently. "He got a double shot of that neurotoxin...he's going to die."

"Please. We need the antidote. We're going to die," Jerry panted desperately.

"Don't sweat it, buddy. What Maschio gave *you* was just water with green food coloring in it," Maschio's Henchman corrected. "The blond one, *he* will die."

Jerry brandished the headless, limbless infant torso in the man's direction.

"Give me the antidote. Now. Or I'll smash it," said Jerry, shaking the infant torso so that it raddled around in its dripping tube.

"So what?" said Maschio's henchman.

"So it won't live outside of its tube."

"I don't believe you. What if the head just grows back?" Maschio's henchman argued.

"The heads don't *grow back*," said Jerry crossly.

"How do you know?"

"I...*uh*...I guess I don't," said Jerry. There were some stories of Strange Lands Lucy in which the monster was decapitated, *and*, as a result, sprouted extra heads.

"The head will grow back," said Machismo's henchman confidently and he reached his hand out of the car window to snatch the surrogate incubator out of Jerry's hands. "Give it here."

Jerry took a step backward and held onto the incubator. The headless torso's breathing had slowed considerably. Perhaps, the thing was dying.

"Give me the antidote now. Or I'll smash the incubator tube and crush the thing inside under my foot until it stops breathing," said Jerry coldly, staring the man down.

"Does it even need to breathe?"

"Want to find out?"

Maschio's henchman groaned, then, opened a suitcase sitting on the passenger seat of the car, and withdrew a hypodermic needle filled with amber fluid.

"Inject him with this before his heart

stops and he will live," said Maschio's henchman, and he put a hand out, intent on receiving the incubator.

"The antidote first," said Jerry.

Maschio's henchman groaned again.

"*Fine*," he said, and then, he handed Jerry the syringe.

Jerry grabbed the syringe, and then, handed Machismo's henchman the incubator. Maschio's henchman grabbed the incubator, rolled up the blacked out window, and sped away, driving off into the distance, and then, out of sight.

<u>13</u>

Jerry ran back to Conrad's car, jumped over the passenger's side door, and landed on the large man's crumpled legs. Conrad twitched slightly in response to the stimulus. His body was trembling almost imperceptibly. His eyes were closed. His mouth was open and dripping.

Jerry grabbed the waist band of Conrad's loose jeans and yanked them down, then, he jabbed the swell of Conrad's behind with the hypodermic needle and injected him with the amber fluid. Conrad's body jerked in response to the stimulus, and then, he went still.

"Fuck...*fuck*...," Jerry swore. Was the syringe that Maschio's henchman had given him just some more poison that would kill Conrad faster?

Jerry got out of the car and paced back and forth a few times in a panic. Conrad's fathers were the two most powerful men in Manazonia. How was he supposed to explain to the two most powerful men in Manazonia that he had just murdered their son?

Conrad stirred. Then, he coughed, as he lifted himself into a sitting position, and wiped the drool off of his open mouth with the back of his hand.

"Uugghh....Jerry?" Conrad murmured groggily, he turned his head and stared at Jerry through squinting, disoriented eyes.

Jerry stopped pacing and turned in Conrad's direction, a look of shock twisting his pale face.

"*Conrad?*"

Conrad's hand shot to his gored shoulder,

pressing his bloodstained shirt to the still dripping wound.

"I'm bleeding out," he murmured groggily, and then, he collapsed backwards onto the front seat of the car again.

Part 3: Lucy's Clue

1

"Fuck," swore Jerry, putting a hand over his own forehead and drawing it down his own cringing face. "*Fuck*....Conrad. I've got to get you to a hospital."

Jerry got back in the car and started to

drive.

"No," Conrad groaned weakly. "No hospital…we're frickin' fugitives now….you fix me."

"What?"

"You said you were trained to do medical stuff," said Conrad. "*You* fix me."

"Are you sure?"

"Yea, and then you can teach me how you did it, like you said. It's probably a skill I could use, anyway," groaned Conrad.

"Fine," said Jerry, staring straight ahead into the distance. "My apartment's a lot closer than the hospital anyway."

2

Louis Ryder was a tall, good-looking man

in his forties with short, grey-flecked, wavy blond hair. He usually had a beverage with him but not because he was thirsty. Beverages were only a prop that he used to appear uninterested in what other people were saying.

"Mr. Ryder, did you get my email?" a balding man with a crooked nose inquired of Louis. This man was a farmer named Roger Harrison; who was responsible for much of the food production in Manazonia.

Louis swiveled his chair around to face the man, lifted a red coffee mug filled with iced late to his parted mouth, and drank from it. He stopped drinking, looked up at the other man as though he were about to speak, and then, instead, drank from the mug again. By forcing his underlings to wait for a reply, Louis continuously reinforced his dominance. It was very important to him that his superior rank never be forgotten.

After some time, Louis put the mug down and replied:

"Yes. I received your email. Please continue."

"There's an East side gang, called the Followers of Polaris," Roger explained. "They've been stealing my produce and reselling it at a decreased price. It's really been cutting into my profits. So...uh...I would really appreciate it if the Company would send some agents to guard my fields...."

Louis lifted the coffee mug to his parted

lips and drank slowly. Then, he put the mug down, stared at Roger for a few moments (as though he were about to speak), and finally, drank from the mug again. Louis put the mug down. He glanced down at his watch. He opened his mouth to speak. Then, he closed his mouth again, got out of his chair, walked over to the espresso machine in the corner of his office, and poured himself another latte. Louis walked back to his chair, slowly inched the coffee mug back up to his parted lips, and then, loudly sipped down its contents.

Roger's left eye was developing a slight twitch, but he knew better than to rush Louis or confront him for being an asshole. Louis had been known to order the executions of those who dared to challenge his dominance.

Louis put the mug down, stared at Roger for a moment, and then, made a small noise in his throat as though he were about to speak. Instead, he picked the mug back up and drank from it again. He drank from it as slowly as was possible. Roger watched with baited breath, wishing the stupid dick would just put the mug down and respond to his question. It had been so long now that Roger had even forgotten what the question had been.

After some time, Louis put down the mug, lifted his head in Roger's direction, and replied coolly: "I'll think about it."

The phone on Louis's desk rang. Louis picked it up and held it to his ear.

"Louis Ryder speaking," he said.

"Louis, it's Rod. Conrad's...*he's*..."

"What, Rodman? This better be damn important," Louis snapped impatiently. As much as he liked to keep people waiting, he hated to be kept waiting himself.

"He's been shot."

<u>3</u>

Jerry quickly removed the gauze from its plastic casing. He glanced down at Conrad, who was stretched out over Jerry's now blood-stained tan sofa, grimacing and clutching his dribbling chest. He was so tall that his feet and calves hung over the side. The sound of Jerry's Dog howling and scratching on the bathroom door (in hopes of being let out into the living room) reverberated off of the walls of the apartment.

"Dio, *sit!*" Jerry commanded the dog harshly. Dio's barks slowed and then faded to reluctant silence.

Jerry knelt down to get on the same level as Conrad's wounds.

"Treating bullet wounds is all about finding the entry point," Jerry said calmly, there was something of that cold, business-like demeanor in this way of speaking. However, the well-practiced ear could detect a subtle faltering in pitch, which betrayed Jerry's conscious control over the way that he spoke. That cold detachedness in his voice did not come naturally.

"First, I'll perform a technique called

scooping, in which I take two fingers," Jerry held up his index and middle finger for Conrad to see. *"Like this.* And scoop the blood out of the leaking wound. This way, I will be able to determine the deeper entry point. This may trigger a severe pain response," he warned.

Jerry dug his fingers into Conrad's seeping wound and began scooping the blood out. Conrad grimaced and squeezed his eyes shut, clamping his teeth down hard and gripping the fabric underneath of him. A strangled groan of pain escaped his tight lips. Dio barked twice, and then, started scratching on the bathroom door again.

Jerry spotted the deeper entry point before the wound filled with blood again. Then, he lifted the gauze. Conrad opened his eyes slightly and stared at it.

"Next," said Jerry. "You take your gauze and do something called *packing*. Always pack in the direction of the deeper wound."

Jerry rolled the end of the gauze into a ball and pushed it into one of the wounds on Conrad's shoulder. Then, he began packing the gushing cavity with the roll of gauze.

"Pack the gauze tightly so that there is no space left inside of the wound," said Jerry as he crumpled what little of the gauze could not be forced into Conrad's wound into a mound. Jerry pressed on the mound of gauze.

"Sit up," he instructed.

Conrad groaned and lifted himself into a

sitting position. Jerry took a second piece of gauze and rapped it around his shoulder and bare chest, securing it in place with a few strips of medical tape. Then, he secured a large, square bandage over the dressed wound.

The door of Jerry's apartment swung open and hit the wall with such force that a decorative glass bowl on Jerry's kitchen counter slid onto the floor and shattered. A row of men, holding rifles, were silhouetted against the bright light in the apartment complex hallway.

"We are agents of The Company!" a man's deep voice boomed threateningly. "Put down your weapons and release the hostage!"

Jerry dropped the roll of gauze he was holding and lifted both of his hands into the air.

He did not turn toward The Company men that stood behind him, but rather, stared down at Conrad, who still had another bullet hole in him that was spewing blood.

"We don't have a hostage," Jerry answered coldly.

"Who is this we? Are there more of you? Release Conrad Ryder if you wish to live!" the man yelled.

"He'll die if you don't let me dress his wound," said Jerry coldly.

"Is that a threat? Cooperate with The Company or you will be terminated!" the man yelled. Dio howled wildly and started scratching on the bathroom door as though he were trying to dig through it.

"Enough! *Enough!* Put down your weapons!" the gruff voice of an older man interjected.

This man must have been of a higher status because as he uttered these words, the others lowered their guns and fell silent, taking a step backward as he walked through their formation outside the door and into the apartment. He switched the brighter light in the foyer on and was revealed to be an unusually tall and broad-shouldered man with a shiny, bald head and a stubble beard. He wore a pair of square, wire-framed glasses, black slacks and a white, button down shirt.

Jerry grabbed the gauze off of the ground and began frantically packing the second bullet wound in Conrad's shoulder with it.

The tall, broad-shouldered man walked over to the edge of the couch, and watched Jerry as he worked.

"Explain yourself," the man said to Jerry as Jerry finished packing the wound, and then, began wrapping more gauze around Conrad's chest and shoulder.

"...Ugh....*Dad?*" Conrad groaned, sounding confused and lightheaded, his eyes flickered shut as another wave of nausea came over him.

"So, you must be Mr. Rodman Ryder," said Jerry coldly. He did not look up to observe the face of the larger man, but rather, stayed focused on what he was doing.

"Explain yourself," Rodman demanded again.

"Conrad and I were taken by The Followers of Maschio. In exchange for our freedom, we were forced to retrieve something for Maschio with a time limit, which prohibited us from filling out the appropriate paperwork to do so," Jerry said.

"Oh," said Rodman suspiciously. There was nothing in his harsh voice to suggest that he believed the story.

"Conrad did what he had to do to survive. Nothing more and nothing less," said Jerry, as he ran out of gauze to rap, and then, began securing it to Conrad's body with medical tape.

"I wouldn't worry about *my son*, there Jack. It's *you* that's going to jail," said Rodman.

Conrad sat up, and groaned, clutching his bandaged chest. Then, stretched and yawned.

"Doesn't hurt," he bragged.

"Conrad, shut up and lay back down," barked Rodman.

Conrad remained upright and glared at him defiantly.

"Jerry's not going to jail," he said, matching Rodman's stern tone.

"Fine. Then you explain what happened here? Why is there a surrogate incubator missing? Why is there a ten car pileup out in front of The Birthing Factory? Why is the *ground* littered with *corpses*?" Rodman ranted furiously.

Conrad explained to Rodman what had happened in detail, and, when *Conrad* told him, he seemed to believe it.

"Maschio will pay for this!" Rodman roared indignantly. "Johnson!"

"Yes, sir!" one of the men outside the door of the apartment barked in reply.

"I want units 9 through 13 working around the clock on the Maschio case. Kill anyone you see swearing their allegiance to him or wearing his colors on sight! I want his gang dismantled! I want his surrogate incubator returned to the birthing factory! I want him detained and publicly executed!"

"Understood, sir!" the men barked back in reply. Then, they turned and exited the hallway, disappearing from sight.

Jerry stood up, observed the irreparable damage to his very expensive couch, and then, shrugged it off, groaning defeated-ly.

"Well, make yourself comfortable. Sit down someplace not bloody, I guess," said Jerry. "I'll get you something to drink."

Jerry walked into the kitchen. He heard the sound of Conrad's father bust out his cell phone and dial someone's number on it. The sound of his voice faded into the background as Jerry's brain filled with static. He felt burnt-out, drained and shriveled like a popped balloon or a deflated pool toy. The sudden absence of adrenaline registered as deadness; emptiness; detachment but not relief.

Jerry retrieved a bottle of wine from one of the kitchen cabinets and filled a couple of glasses. He then returned to the living room, clutching a wine glass in both hands. The front door burst open again, and an attractive man with wavy blond hair stepped into the room.

"Conrad!" the man greeted cheerfully.

"Pops?" Conrad murmured in reply.

"I'll take that," said the blond man and he grabbed both wine glasses out of Jerry's hands and drank them both down in under five seconds. He handed the empty glasses back to Jerry as though presenting trash to a servant. "Be a pal and go fetch some more."

"Uh. Right. Of course Mr…"

"Louis Ryder," said the man.

"Louis Ryder himself, huh?" said Jerry, trying to sound impressed but failing due to his mental tiredness. He trudged back into the kitchen.

"And something to eat too! I'm starved," Louis shouted.

Jerry returned to the kitchen. He took the bottle of wine back out of the cabinet, then, went to the refrigerator, and retrieved a plastic container filled with left over cheese raviolis and a white carton of Chinese take out rice. He dumped these two things in a plate, and then, dumped the plate in the microwave.

"So, now that I've seen the birthing factory, I have to ask. Which one of you is related to me genetically?" Jerry heard Conrad ask.

"We *both* are.   When a Manazonian couple applies for a child, the birthing factory takes sperm samples from both of them and mixes them together.   Then, inseminates the surrogate incubator with both samples," explained Louis.

"I just wish you had gone to the authorities instead of breaking into that place," said Rodman to Conrad. He found a blood free place to sit, on the coffee table between the couch and the TV.   Then, sat down on it, crossing his arms.

Louis stretched out his arm, and knocked a stack of painted canvases off of a stool by the couch, as though brushing dust off of something unclean. Then, he sat down as well.

"Well that's no fun," said Louis.

"Louis, *I swear to God*," Rodman growled.

"Is my car trashed?" Conrad inquired
morosely.

"Yea, I drove past it on the way here,"
said Louis. "It got wrecked to shit."

"Fuck," Conrad swore.

"Don't sweat it, Conrad. I'll get you a
new one," said Luis.

"No you fucking won't," said Rodman,
pointing at Louis with an accusing finger.

Jerry returned to the living room with a
tray of food. He gave a bowl of day-old raviolis
mixed with white rice to each man, and then,
poured them each a glass of wine.

"What kind of a car do you want?" Louis asked Conrad, ignoring Rodman's comment.

"Uh...," Conrad murmured uncomfortably. To answer was to take a side.

"This is your problem, Louis! You always coddle him! He blows up half the city and your first reaction is to buy him a car!" Rodman shouted angrily.

Louis grinned and sipped the wine from his glass slowly, while Rodman fumed. Then, he lowered the glass.

"He's been through a traumatic experience," Louis said calmly.

"He's a grown-ass man. He can buy his own damn car," growled Rodman.

Jerry took a few steps backward. He

watched as Conrad and his fathers ate, but did not eat anything himself.

"Conrad, I'm buying you *two* cars," announced Louis, smirking defiantly. "And a fuckin' jet! And some more guns. Do you need more guns, Conrad?"

"He's got enough guns, Louis," said Rodman, with irritation, but again his comment went ignored.

"Uh…yea, whatever," said Conrad, shoveling forkfuls of raviolis and white rice into his open mouth. He chewed them quickly, and then, swallowed. "I like cool shit." He shoved more food into his mouth, chewed, then swallowed it. Then, he said: "Can I get like, one of those giant monster trucks with wheels that're like ten-feet high? And like, I don't know. A fuckin' motorcycle?"

"I thought we agreed you've wrecked enough motorcycles," said Rodman. Again, his comment went ignored.

"Well you can't be a proper dude-bro without a motorcycle, can you?" mused Louis, grinning. "Sure, son. Why the fuck not?"

"Why the fuck not indeed," Rodman groaned defeated-ly.

"You there, *what's your face!*" Louis shouted, addressing Jerry as "what's your face." "Order me some fucking....some fucking pizza or something. I don't believe that you have the audacity to serve us *this* shit. Do you know who I am, little man? I might as well be your fucking

king!"

Louis shoved the bowl of food back in Jerry's direction, and Jerry took it out of his hands with out saying a word, as Luis Ryder was known for having those who challenged his dominance executed.

"*Hey*!" Conrad boomed, locking eyes on the blonder of his two fathers. "You don't talk to *him* like *that*! ...*Ever*! You got that?"

Luis chuckled.

"Oh *I* see how it is," he said, smiling knowingly.

"Stop that," grumbled Conrad. "Stop smiling."

"I know what's going on here," said Louis, his smirk un-flickering.

"Jerry, you have a uh…an interesting collection of paintings here," said Rodman, observing the painting on the wall, dividing the kitchen from the living room.

"Thank you," replied Jerry coldly. He returned to the living room.

"Where'd you get them?" Rodman inquired conversationally.

"I painted them," Jerry replied.

"Really?" said Rodman, sounding impressed. "They're very good."

"Thank you," replied Jerry.

"When I was a lad, I was interested in painting myself," said Rodman. "But I was never very good at capturing people. Mostly, I just painted landscapes."

"Nonsense, I'm sure you could paint anything you want to, sir," said Jerry robotically. He did not much like the idea of making Rodman Ryder angry, as the man had the authority to execute anyone at any time that he chose.

Rodman laughed and shook his head.

"Sadly, that was never the case," he said. Then, he put his fork in what remained of the rice in his bowl, and put the bowl down on the coffee table next to him.

"You're very talented," Rodman said to Jerry politely.

"Thank you, sir," replied Jerry cautiously.

Rodman glanced over at Conrad who was still shoveling food in his mouth. His bandaged chest rose and fell with slow deliberate breaths as he willed the signs of pain off of his face with well practiced skill. Then, Rodman glanced back at Jerry, whose thick glasses caught the light overhead, obscuring his eyes from view. Jerry stared back, frowning.

"...Sir?" Jerry inquired, confused by Rodman's long silence.

"Please," Rodman said, and he stuck his hand out for Jerry to shake. "Call me Dad."

4

Jerry thought he felt his heart stop in his chest, and then, for a moment, he lost the ability to breathe. It was as though a phantom hand were strangling him; crushing his windpipe beneath broad, angry fingertips and causing the blood to rush to his head, the pressure behind his eyes building steadily. What exactly did Rodman mean by that? *Call me Dad...* Was the man really anticipating having Jerry as a son-in-law? Jerry sucked in air. Exhaled slowly, and then, shook Rodman's outstretched hand.

The next day, Jerry woke up, showered, dressed, and then, leashed Dio for a walk. Dio panted heavily and his lips curled into a fanged smile as his bushy tail wagged from side to side. Jerry began to think about Lucy's clue: the folded piece of paper taped to the underside of the surrogate incubator's tube. Then, about what Conrad's father had said to him last night.

Jerry walked Dio to the end of the hallway and into the elevator, then, pushed the first floor button. The elevator doors slid shut and the machine made a sharp *ding* noise, as it began to descend slowly. The image of Rodman, sitting on the coffee table, stretching out his hand for Jerry to shake, forced itself back into Jerry's head. ...*Call me Dad,* the mental image insisted.

"Fuck," Jerry swore under his breath, drawing the palm of his hand slowly over his hot forehead and sweating face. "Fuck. Fuck. Fuck. Fuck me. Fuck my life."

The elevator made another sharp *ding* noise. The doors slid open. Jerry forced his expression to resemble that of an emotionless mask. Then, stepped out of the elevator and into the apartment lobby. Jerry walked Dio past a hotel door man sitting behind a counter, a row of ferns, and a couple of plush green-upholstery chairs. Then, he walked through the revolving glass door and out to the street. Here, cars inched by slowly, encumbered by traffic and swarms of pedestrians. Every so often, Jerry heard a man in a car slam his hand down on his car horn and yell profanity at the pedestrians or another driver.

"Jerry, good morning," Churchill greeted as he walked up to him. Churchill had his long, curly-black hair tied up in a pony tail and was wearing a black sweatshirt and grey sweatpants. He was also walking a rat-sized black Chihuahua with a white stripe down the center of his head, and a rapidly flailing white-tipped tail.

"Danny, hey," Jerry greeted unenthusiastically and he waved.

The two dogs sniffed each other, wagging their tails rapidly.

"I heard that Conrad was injured in the line of duty," said Churchill.

The two men began to walk together.

"Well, of course you did. You hear everything," said Jerry.

"He didn't come to work on Friday," said Churchill. "But then again, neither did you."

"Uh…yea, I needed a mental health day," said Jerry.

"Feeling a touch overwhelmed?"

"Eh...you know, man," Jerry shrugged as

he struggled to find the words he would need to communicate exactly what his problem was. "I'm just trying to claw my way out of this pile of shit I'm under."

"Indeed," Churchill commiserated. "The job can have that effect on some people. It is my understanding that you worked for The Company as a clerk, and later, as a police sketch artist. Do you think you would be happier doing that kind of thing again, Jerry?"

"Yea, probably," said Jerry, shrugging. "But what can you do?"

"It is also my understanding that, while you were being held captive by Maschio, he showed you his face."

"Is that so unusual?" Jerry inquired.

"Maschio has never shown anyone his face. That's why he's so hard to capture. Nobody knows what he looks like," explained Churchill.

"So you're saying that I should sketch Maschio's face?"

"I'm saying that when you go back to work on Monday, they're going to *make* you sketch his face. I'm only suggesting that you start now while the image is fresh in your mind," said Churchill.

The two men reached the corner of the block. The traffic lights were green and a solid wall of slow moving cars obstructed their progress.

Jerry groaned.

"I don't think I want to relive that nightmare right now," he said. Then, he thought of Lucy's clue again: the folded piece of paper, now sitting in his pocket. Jerry's fear that the paper was actually nothing and therefore pointless was keeping the thing folded and un-looked at for the moment.

"Understandable," said Churchill. "But for the sake of conversation, what was the man like?"

The traffic light turned red and the cars stopped. Jerry and Churchill crossed the street. They kept walking.

"He was...uh....I don't know how to explain this...uh....oddly preoccupied with my opinion of him," said Jerry.

"You mean was he vain? I suppose that makes sense," said Churchill.

"Yea, well, I mean he was vain, but he was also very uh....*obsessed* with me, I guess. I mean, this guy wanted to hump my brains out. It was creepy as fuck," said Jerry.

"I've heard a lot about Maschio and his gang, over the years," said Churchill. "And I'll concede it is very strange that he showed you his face and made it clear who he was. He's known for not doing that."

"Maybe it was just a henchman that Maschio sent to pose as him?" said Jerry.

"I find that more likely," said Churchill and he stretched, yawning. "But, who knows? Stranger things have happened."

"Has Wyatt Parker's apartment been searched yet?" Jerry asked as the two men continued to walk.

"Excuse me?"

"Wyatt Parker's apartment. The computer department, traced Ms. Lucy's email to..." Jerry groaned, brushing his bangs away from his aching forehead. "Oh Christ. I don't even have the energy this morning..."

"Actually, there was an apartment searched in association with that Ms. Lucy email. The investigation was made during the time that you were being held captive by Maschio's gang," said Churchill.

"Yea?"

"The place is now the residence of

Wyatt's Parker's cousin, Laurence Dresden. Dresden was taken in and questioned but as of yet has not divulged any information pertinent to the Lucy case. The apartment was turned over by agents but so far, no clues relating to Lucy's whereabouts have been found."

"There must be something there," Jerry said.

"Unfortunately, there does not appear to be."

"What about Conrad? How's he doing?" Jerry asked.

"How should I know? I haven't seen him for some time."

"Well, I was under the impression that you know everything."

Churchill sighed and shook his head.

"Well, if you must know," Churchill conceded. "Conrad's been shot and stabbed and burned in the line of duty before. He's pretty hard to slow down. I remember this one time, this monster got into Manazonia from The Strange Lands and it smashed Conrad's ribs basically to powder. But nothing slows that kid down. He just keeps fighting and fighting and fighting and fighting. It's the way he's programmed. He was born and bread to be a war machine."

"A war machine, huh?" Jerry mused. An image of Conrad flashed in his mind. The massive, bull-like man seemed almost twice Jerry's height and his thick muscular arms glistened with perspiration as he lifted a two hundred pound weights over his spiky blond head. "…Yea. I can see that."

<h2 style="text-align:center"><u>5</u></h2>

That night, Conrad dreamed about Lucy. She was on the bridge in the park again. She turned away from Conrad, her head hidden beneath a lacy pink umbrella. It wasn't raining but the sky was overcast. Conrad sprinted over to Lucy, his chest burning as though it had been set on fire and pounding as though it had been beaten. Lucy moved slowly away from him and did not turn to acknowledge his presence.

"Lucy, Lucy….*wait!*" Conrad shouted.

Lucy did not speak nor did she turn around.

Conrad took a step closer to her. Lucy took a step of identical length forward.

Conrad was quiet for a moment. He stood very still and listened to the rain as it began to fall and gather in puddles around his feet. Lucy was quiet as well and did not turn. Conrad stared at the back of her sunflower yellow head and watched its golden strands as they began to blow in the growing storm. Then, Lucy turned, her face was a bloody, featureless pit and she screamed, flinging herself at Conrad and ripping his still beating heart from his body with her long, pink fingernails.

Conrad's eyes shot open and he sat upright. He got out of bed, lifted the mattress, and found the illegal naked picture of the shman that he kept hidden there. The shman stared up at him through heavily painted eyelids. She wore a randy, starved expression that suggested she were about to jump off of the page and fuck Conrad silly.

Conrad took the picture of the shman with him to the bathroom. His fingers slipped below the waste band of his boxers and he imagined himself caress the creature in the photograph with a confused, sexually voracious embrace.

When, at last, he had finished, he put the picture down on the edge of the bathroom sink and stared at his own face in the mirror. A wave of shame crashed over him. How could he have gotten so aroused by one of those bizarre walking incubators?

Conrad exited the bathroom and walked back to the kitchen. He opened the mostly empty refrigerator and retrieved a beer. Then, snapped the top open, tilted his head backward, and quickly drained its contents. He retrieved a second beer, opened it, and took a long, slow, deep, drag from it.

He found his cell phone in the bedroom, unplugged it from its charger, and dialed Jerry's number. It rang several times, and then, someone picked up.

"Jerry?" Conrad murmured.

"...*Conrad*, it's two in the morning! *What the fuck?*" Conrad heard Jerry's tired voice rage indignantly.

"I can't sleep," Conrad said quietly.

"So what do you want me to do about it?"

"Uh..."

"Go to sleep, Conrad," Jerry groaned.

"...You said that Lucy would leave a clue on incubator 9999," Conrad said. "Well...did he?"

Jerry was silent for a moment.

"Jerry?"

"Yea, actually. She did. But we can talk about that in the morning," said Jerry.

"No. Let's talk about it now."

"There was a piece of paper taped to the underside of the tube. You probably didn't see it because you were losing consciousness and everything. But, yea. It was definitely there," said Jerry.

"What does it say?"

"Huh?"

"The paper that Lucy left, what does it say?" Conrad asked.

"Well...um....I don't really know," conceded Jerry, sounding a bit embarrassed. "I haven't looked at it yet."

"*What*? Why not?"

"I don't fucking know, because I need a break from this shit maybe?" Jerry snapped rather defensively. "What if it's nothing? It could just be nothing, right?"

"Yea....I guess. But what if it's, you know, something?" Conrad proposed with baited breath. What if Lucy was real? What if

Jerry held the clue that would lead them to her? Conrad imagined himself reach out and touch one of the floppy appendages protruding from the shman in the photograph's chest. It felt cool. Like a hard stone smoothed round by the tides the ocean. Conrad pushed the thought out of his head. The thought reasserted itself promptly. Sure his mission was to exterminate the monster but who was going to know whether or not he fooled around with it first? Nobody. That was who.

"I don't know, do you think I should unfold it now?" Jerry said.

"Uh...sure," said Conrad quickly. "Unfold it."

"Or maybe I should just leave it alone and

hand it over to The Company tomorrow."

"No, don't do that," said Conrad earnestly. "They already think you're a joke. This is your chance to show them what you can do. Plus, I'm technically supposed to be on sick leave right now, so if it's a map or something and they send you out into The Strange Lands, they'll send you out with a new partner."

"So?"

"So, I've worked on this too long not to see it play out," asserted Conrad. "I intend to kill Lucy myself. After all we've been through, I'll be damned if I'm going to let some other schmuck get the credit for it." Conrad slammed his fist down on the bedside table for emphasis.

Jerry laughed.

"What about your shoulder wounds?" he asked, and Conrad could hear the grin on Jerry's face, because the man was already anticipating what Conrad was about to say.

"Shoulder wounds?" Conrad scoffed. "Who cares! I an't gonna die!"

Jerry laughed again.

"It takes a whole lot more than that to slow you down, huh Buddy?" Jerry observed drolly.

"An't nothin' gonna slow us down!" Conrad bragged triumphantly. "That little dick-less bastard is as good as dead!"

"Fuck yea! We got this!" Jerry exclaimed, getting caught up in Conrad's enthusiasm.

"I've killed monsters bigger than sky

scrapers, bigger'n my dick even! Killing this Lucy thing'll be easy!" said Conrad.

"And then we get a fat bonus check for Lucy's head on a platter!" Jerry exclaimed excitedly. He began thinking about what he would do with the extra money. Perhaps he would buy a car; a big, black truck with massive tires that he would use to transport nothing. Or perhaps he would move into a better apartment, a bigger apartment with a better view, a closet full of designer suits, and amazing shower pressure.

"It's going to be the best," said Conrad.

"There's literally no way we could fail," Jerry agreed.

"Hey, Jerry?"

"Yea?"

"Don't unfold that paper without me, ok?" Conrad said. "It's going to be like…like fucking *Christmas morning*."

"Yea….yea, ok, man. You got it," agreed Jerry.

"Goodnight, Jerry."

"….Goodnight, Conrad."

Conrad turned his cell phone off and fell backwards onto his bed, beaming as though he were in love. His eyes slid shut and he fell into a deep and trouble-less sleep.

6

Jerry's now couch-less living room was lit by the warm glow of the morning sun. Through the large window on the wall were the couch used to sit, the city skyline was visible, silhouetted by the orange light of dawn.

Someone knocked on the door. Dio began to bark and wag his tail rapidly as he trotted towards the source of the noise.

"Who is it?" Jerry called from the kitchen. He was staring at his coffee machine as it began to make a slow, quiet, hissing noise, and produce a stream of dark brown liquid.

"It's Conrad!" Conrad's voice boomed from behind the door.

"Uh, right! Yea...Just a second!" Jerry called back. He sprinted to the bathroom, dumped his blue bathrobe on the floor, and then, dressed himself quickly in a pair of tan slacks and a white button down shirt. Then, he walked to the front door of his apartment and let Conrad in.

Dio sprinted toward Conrad, panting excitedly and he launched himself into the air, hitting Conrad in the stomach with his front paws.

"Hey, doggy," Conrad said to the dog as it landed on the floor and jumped a second time, hitting Conrad in the stomach with his front paws again. Conrad stretched his arm out and mussed the dog's long, pointed ears with the palm of his hand.

Dio seemed to be satisfied by this, because his panting slowed and he lost interest in Conrad. Then, he trotted off to the bathroom, were he curled up in a ball on top of Jerry's robe.

"Still have that piece of paper?" Conrad asked Jerry.

"Yea," said Jerry, sounding a bit hesitant. He held up the folded piece of paper for Conrad to see. "It's right here."

"And you didn't look at it yet?" Conrad asked.

"No," said Jerry. "I waited for you. Like you wanted."

"Sweet," said Conrad, grinning. "Let's open it."

Jerry walked to the square white table in the kitchen and sat down. Then, he sat the folded piece of paper down on the surface in front of him. Conrad sat down in the chair across from him and watched as the smaller man unfolded the paper with shaking hands.

There appeared to be two pieces of paper in the bundle. The one top was a typed letter. Jerry lifted it off of the table to read, revealing the second piece of paper underneath. This was a detailed map of The Strange Lands annotated in certain places with red pen.

"Dear Reader," Jerry read. His voice was quiet and even but his fingers gripped the letter with unnecessary force that threatened to crinkle it. "Enclosed is a map, which will lead you to Strange Lands Lucy, the only intact woman alive today. Please, use this map only if you intend to join The Cult of Lucy, and with the understanding that those who come without this intention do so at their own peril. Note also please, that Miss Lucy does not accept parties of men larger than three. Groups of four or larger will be gunned down on sight. Please arrive on foot or by terrain vehicle. All helicopters and aerial crafts will be shot down on sight.

To show your support for The Cult of Lucy, we request that you bring with you an offering of food rations, water, weapons, ammo, clothing, blankets, vehicles, money and/or cut flowers. Note please, that Lucy will reward offerings based on their quantity and usefulness and in the form of physical intimacy up to and including full sexual intercourse. Though all offerings are appreciated, please note that larger offerings will yield greater rewards.

Your Brother in Arms,

Brendan of The Cult of Lucy"

Jerry put the paper back down just as Conrad picked up the map and began to examine it.

"I don't get maps," said Conrad, as he observed the incomprehensible network of rivers and caves and mountains, which crisscrossed the Strange Lands.

"Let me see it," Jerry said.

Conrad turned the map sideways and squinted.

Jerry walked over to him and ripped the map out of his hands.

"*Hey!*" Conrad complained.

Jerry stared down at the map. He had taken a class on map reading and felt comfortable enough reading the red pen annotations that were scribbled in the margins.

"Yup," said Jerry. "This is a map alright. And if the letter is telling the truth…it should lead us straight to her."

"Well…better start collecting my offering," said Conrad. He stood up and started walking toward the door.

"You're bringing an offering?" Jerry commented incredulously as he watched Conrad leave.

Conrad turned back around and, to defend this choice, explained: "Yea, if we don't bring one, they'll be suspicious, won't they?"

"Well…I *suppose* that's true," Jerry conceded.

"And it'll be easy for us to kill her if they leave us alone with her," said Conrad. "So, bigger offerings are better.

"Right," Jerry conceded. "But if your offer's too big they might suspect that your offering is government funded."

"Oh. Ok. Noted," said Conrad quickly.

He walked back to the table and grabbed the map.

"We should bring this back to headquarters now," said Conrad. "See what kind of an offering they hook us up with."

"Sure, ok," said Jerry far less enthusiastically. He was not sure he understood that amorous glint in Conrad's eyes; that predatory grin. *Conrad can't be thinking about fooling around with that monster before he kills it, can he?*, Jerry thought uncomfortably.

Jerry and Conrad left the apartment. Jerry folded the letter from Lucy up and stuck it in the pocket of his tan slacks. Conrad kept staring at the map of The Strange Lands and trying to make sense of it.

"Conrad, put that away before someone sees you holding it," Jerry said with some degree of exasperation as he and Conrad walked from the apartment building to Conrad's new car, which was double parked in a pair of handicapped spaces, near the front of a parking lot, across the street. It was a massive black monster truck with tall wheels, chrome hubcaps, and flames painted down the sides of it. There were a couple of reclined, muscular men, in silhouette, printed on the mud flaps.

"Just a second, I'm looking at it," said Conrad as they continued to walk toward the car.

A crowd of pedestrians walked with them along the sidewalk.

"You can read it later," said Jerry earnestly. "Put it away."

"No," said Conrad defiantly.

"Goddamn it, Conrad, put it away," Jerry growled.

A man wearing black clothes and a black ski mask emerged from the crowd and ripped the map out of Conrad's hands. Conrad, who had not been expecting this, took a few seconds longer than was optimal to register what had happened.

"Shit!" he swore.

"After him!" Jerry yelled.

Jerry and Conrad sprinted after the man with the ski mask. The thief had long spidery legs and moved a like a black shadow, weaving through the oncoming crowd of boisterous pedestrians with grace and ease. He out ran both Jerry and Conrad easily, and made it to the parking lot in front of Jerry's apartment, before either of them were able to cross the street.

He ran to a scratched and dented white vehicle with a cracked windshield, unlocked the driver's side door, jumped in, and sped away. Jerry and Conrad reached the parking lot. They bolted toward Conrad's massive truck, climbed inside, and sped after the thief, who was, by this point, a little more than a two blocks away. Scowling with determination, Conrad slammed his foot down on the gas and tore out of the parking lot. Several dozen pedestrians screamed as they darted out of the way to avoid being crushed flat beneath the treads of four massive monster truck wheels. The dented white car was visible now, a mere eight or nine feet away from the front of the monster truck's grill. Conrad sped up and so did the thief. Then, the thief took a sharp turn. Conrad did the same, but his large truck did not turn as easily as the thief's small car, and there was lag. The thief sped further into the distance. Conrad weaved around a few speed-limit-observing cars, and through a red traffic light, in a four way intersection. The shrill beeping of men slamming their fists against car horns rang in Conrad's ears, followed by the loud *skreeee* of squeaking breaks. Then, there was the sound of shattering glass and crushing metal that must have been the resulting car crash.

Conrad could see the white car again now, it was a mere ten or so inches from the grill of his speeding monster truck. Then, without any warning at all, the white car took a sharp left turn. Conrad attempted to imitate the abrupt movement, but his reaction time was too slow, and the truck was moving too quickly. So, instead, Conrad's massive truck skid over a short stretch of sidewalk and dry dead grass, then, slammed grill-first into the windowless brick back of a tall building. Jerry screamed and covered his face with his hands as the windshield shattered inward and sprayed them both with glass.

The two were quiet for a moment. Conrad squinted and tried to blink beads of shattered safety glass out of his small eyes.

"That fucking *son of man whore*!" he yelled and he slammed his large fist against the wheel of the truck, causing the horn to blow long and hard.

The sound of the horn faded to nothing and Conrad took a few slow deep breaths, and then, asked in a much calmer voice: "Jerry, are you alright?"

"Yea," Jerry replied quietly. "You?"

"Yea, I'm fine," said Conrad, and then, he added in a much more depressed tone. "I can't believe that happened. I'm such a fucking..." Conrad slammed his fist down on the car horn again. "*Idiot!*"

"...Conrad," Jerry murmured.

"We almost had it. Strange Lands Lucy was as good as *dead*!"

"Conrad!" Jerry interrupted and he shoved a paper napkin from the Lardo's Baccon Hut in Conrad's face.

Conrad blinked and stared at the number written on the napkin.

"I wrote his license plate number down,"

Jerry explained with some degree of irritation.

Conrad grinned. Then, through his head back and laughed heartily.

"The company will find him and retrieve the map," Jerry said. "It's only a matter of time."

"*Yea*, they will," Conrad agreed, and he started to chuckle again. In his post-traumatic elated state, he almost reached the point of hysteria. What Jerry had said was true. The Company would hunt the thief down and take that map back. It was only a matter of time.

7

Churchill turned his computer chair in the direction of the interrogation room. A slender, dark-haired man with long, skinny legs and a sharp, curved nose stared back at him.

The man was naked and bloody. His body trembled with every slow rattling breath and perspiration dotted his sloping forehead. This man's name was Johnny Davis and he was the thief who had taken Lucy's Strange Lands map. He had been easy enough to catch. The Company was the sole distributor of license plates in Manazonia and each license plate contained within it, a tracking device, which could be activated by entering the license plate number into the Company database. A fleet of Company Men had been waiting for Johnny when he arrived back at his apartment, but, by then, the thief had already gotten rid of the map.

"Where did you hide Lucy's map?" Churchill asked the man detachedly.

"I....I told you....," the man gasped between deep, heaving breaths. "I destroyed it."

"Liar," Churchill remarked nonchalantly. Then, he pushed a button on his remote. A pair of robotic hands emerged from the ceiling of the room and grabbed the trembling thief by his wrists. A second pair of robotic hands sprang from the floor and grabbed this man by his ankles.

"Fine then, don't tell me just yet," said Churchill as though he were having a relaxed discussion with a friend over tea. "I welcome the opportunity to utilize my new machine. You see, traditional Chinese medicine has always fascinated me, Johnny. Particularly, acupuncture. *Acupuncture*, incase you don't know, is the art of sticking needles in pressure points in the human body to relieve pain and cure ailments. And the idea of it got me thinking, could inserting needles in the right pressure points of the human body, produce the *opposite* effect? Might...it be possible to locate and identify clusters of nerves that, when pierced by a needle, produce extreme pain and other deleterious effects, such as headaches, nausea, loss of bowel control etcetera, etcetera, and so on and so forth? The question lead me to pursue the research and the research led to the invention of the machine that you're attached to. If you fail to cooperate with the company, you will experience something like acupuncture, Johnny, except in reverse. I call it...acu*fuck*ture."

"*Fuck you*," Johnny spat.

"Where's the map?" Churchill asked again.

"I destroyed it," Johnny murmured back, determinately.

Churchill pushed a button on his remote and a pair of syringes sprang from the ceiling, impaling Johnny's glistening neck on both sides. Johnny screamed in pain.

"Where's the map, Johnny? Why did you steal the map?" Churchill asked calmly.

"....I....oh   God.....*Lucy!*"   Johnny screamed. His body convulsed as he attempted to pull away from the needles but with no avail. Then, he began raving, speaking to Strange Lands Lucy as though she were some kind of an omniscient deity. "Lucy...my love! *I'll protect you! We....we'll be together soon...."*

Churchill nodded. His prisoner's outburst had given him an idea.

"It couldn't possibly hurt your precious Lucy to tell me how and why you stole the map. I must admit, I am curious. So let's say. That...if you tell me everything, I will remove the needles from your neck," said Churchhill into the microphone on his desk.

"F...forgive me, *Lucy*," Johnny gasped in reply. *"Take the needles out first!"*

"Very well," Churchill said and he pushed a button on his remote. The needles were pulled out of the man's neck and he breathed a slow, rattling sigh of relief. The needles remained poised at the sides of his bloody neck, ready to re-imbed themselves should he anger Churchill again.

"I...oh....*oh God!*" Johnny wept. "F...forgive me Lucy....I....I found a folder filled with Company files....they said that Lucy was real and that she was alive...and I had always felt that Lucy was alive...that she was somewhere out there...w-waiting for me...and that she would love me after I found her...that she loves me now. I-I have always felt that....Lucy thinks about me the way that I think about her...."

"You specifically?" Churchill inquired, a bit amused by the weeping man's incredible narcissism. How could Lucy be in love with a person that she did not know existed?

"Yes...," Johnny confirmed. "I know it's stupid...but Lucy....she must think about me...she must....they say s-she has...a woman's intuition...it's like having telepathy or s-something. She had visions of me, and she can see me, and she knows how much I love her. She must. When I speak to her...s-she hears me. Sometimes I even hear her answering me back..."

"Johnny, it says in your file that you've spent many years in a mental institution for latent heterosexual tendencies, hallucinations, psychotic episodes, and delusions of grandeur. Is that true?" Churchill inquired, though of course he knew the answer was "yes."

"Yea, it's true," the man yelled back. "But I'm not crazy! Lucy is real! *She's real!* And she *loves me*! She's waiting for me!"

"I wonder, Johnny? Was your theft of the map a happy accident? To me, that seems rather unlikely," said Churchill.

"No...it wasn't an accident...after I found the files...L-lucy....she told me to keep an eye on The Company Men. So I did...There's like seven or eight guys who live near my apartment and work for The Company...so I found out where they all live and planted bugs in their apartments."

"So you had Jerry Cosco's apartment bugged?" Churchill inquired.

"Yea, and several others," confessed

Johnny stupidly. "I heard that Jerry guy talking to his buddy about the map, so I drove over there and waited outside of the apartment for them to walk out with it."

"Fascinating. I dare say you'd be an impressive man if you weren't such a raving loon," remarked Churchill.

"I told you I'm not crazy!"

"Crazy is as crazy does, Mr. Davis," Churchill said boredly. Then, he yawned and pushed a couple of buttons on his remote. The needles rammed themselves back into the sides of Johnny's raw, gushing neck. While at the same time, a second pair of needles emerged from the ceiling and penetrated the skin on his forehead. Johnny screamed and screamed and his body convulsed. Grotesque rivulets of tears and snot spilled from his eyes and nose over his shrieking, blood-splattered face. He began to rave again, declaring his love for Strange Lands Lucy; swearing as though she were standing before him that he would find her one day.

"Lucy!" Johnny shrieked, as though addressing some invisible third person standing between him and Churchill. "We will fulfill the prophecy! ...And, *lo*, Nothing can prevent the union of Lucy with her lover, the man who will be *king* of the new world! Woman born of woman will be conceived under the light of the red moon! Nothing can prevent the birth of this monster, for she and she alone will have the power to *slay The Overlords*!"

Churchill shook his head dismissively. It annoyed him slightly that Johnny shrieked the prophecy espoused by The Cult of Lucy as though it were a personal threat.

"Yes, yes, I've heard it all before," said Churchill indifferently. Then, he pushed a button on his remote and sent a jolt of electricity through the needles and into Johnny's wildly convulsing body. The man screamed, then, babbled some more nonsense about Lucy. Then, he screamed again.

For three months, Johnny Davis was tortured in this way. Until finally, having suffered innumerably and irreversibly, the man lost all hope of ever escaping, retrieving the hidden map, and impregnating Strange Lands

Lucy, as he had once planned. With the promise that the torture would, at long last, be over forever, he confessed that he had hidden Lucy's map under a loose floorboard in his apartment, before being captured by government agents and brought to The Company. Then, Johnny Davis, having exhausted his usefulness, was transferred from his interrogation cell to a padded room in a high security mental institution.

The map was then retrieved by agents of The Company and delivered to the office of Louis and Rodman Ryder.

8

There was an executive desk toy on Louis's desk, a row of silver balls hanging from translucent strings, which, when tapped, made a *clink, clink, clink, clink* noise. Louis played with the executive desk toy frequently and for two reasons: A) because it made his underlings feel unimportant when they were trying to talk to him, and B) because Louis was mesmerized by its constant motion. His compulsion to keep making those silver balls clink together was far too powerful to be ignored for very long.

Clink, clink, clink, clink, the silver balls on the executive desk toy clanked together. Louis tapped them again and they clacked faster.

Rodman handed Lucy's map to Conrad.

"You sure you want to do this, son? I could very easily get someone else for this mission," he said.

"Don't sweat it, Dad, my shoulder's pretty much healed," said Conrad, grinning as he observed the map in his hands. Having been raised in the age of the GPS, he could not read the thing. To him, it was just a colorful mess of lines and dots.

"Can you even read a map?" Rodman asked skeptically. His expression was a mixture of incredulity and concern.

"Nah," Conrad admitted, waving a hand dismissively. Then, he shrugged. "But you know, psh. Whatever."

"You tell 'im, Conrad, maps 're stupid!" Louis said from his desk. His eyes were still glued to the executive desk toy as it clanked and clanked.

Rodman groaned and put a hand over his face.

"Well, you *need* to be able to read a map, Conrad," said Rodman.

"Can't yer little friend, whats-is-face read maps?" Louis asked. Again, not finding the conversation important enough to take his eyes off of the executive desk toy.

"Jerry, yea. He said that he can read maps," said Conrad.

"Jerry's not good in a fight, Conrad, and Lucy will be well guarded. It would be smart to take a couple of soldiers from the infantry. I assure you, they'll both know how to read maps," said Rodman.

"Well, I'm taking Jerry," said Conrad, as

though he were talking about a formal dance and not an assassination mission.

Louis sighed, while somehow still managing to sound uninterested by what they were talking about.

"Conrad, you can pal around with your stupid boyfriend after you come back from the mission," Louis said. The executive desk toy stopped clinking and Louis tapped it to start the incessant clinking again.

"What, you think he's not good enough to go on this mission?" Conrad replied with a bit of irritation.

"...Conrad," Rodman sighed in exasperation.

"Because he's more than good enough,"

Conrad growled, tapping Rodman on the chest with his index finger. However, the two men were exactly the same height and Rodman was not intimidated. He stared back at his son with a look of exasperation, then, took a deep slow breath to calm himself and said in an even voice:

"Conrad, when we decide who goes on these missions, it's important to understand that our men are tools. And, like a mechanic working on a car, The Overlords use a variety of different tools to keep society rolling."

"Is this going somewhere?" Conrad interrupted with irritation.

"Yes, Conrad."

"Because I'm getting sick of this conversation already."

"Conrad, my point is this: *not every tool is good for every job*. For instance, if I'm fixing something and it has a loose screw. I'm going to use a screw driver. If I try to use a wrench to fix a loose screw, it just won't get fixed. If I'm tightening a loose bolt, on the other hand, I'm going to use a wrench. Guess what'll happen if I try to use a screwdriver? It *won't* get fixed. You see, both a wrench and a screwdriver have a purpose, just because I choose one over the other for a specific job doesn't really make one more important than the other."

"Uh huh. And what's your point again?" Conrad interrupted.

"Conrad, Jerry is like a wrench. This mission is a like a loose screw. And The

Overlords don't need a wrench to fix this problem. They need a screw driver. So, when I say Jerry's not good for this mission, I'm not passing judgment on your friend or saying that he's lacking in anyway. I'm just saying that he's not the right man for this particular job. Jerry's a wrench. This job needs a screw driver," explained Rodman.

"Uh huh," said Conrad, rather disinterestedly. "So I can take Jerry, right?"

"Conrad, did you listen to anything I just said?" Rodman asked.

"Sure," said Conrad.

"What did I just say?"

"You said that there's a wrench and a screw driver and blah blah blah The Overlords need tools, so we're all tools and some other shit. Yea. I don't care. I'm taking Jerry," said Conrad.

"Louis, are you listening to this?" Rodman groaned, shaking his head.

"So he wants to take the little guy?" Louis said from his desk, eyes still glued on the executive desk toy. "Let him take the little guy."

Part 4: The Strange Lands

<u>1</u>

Manazonia was surrounded by a vast and monster-infested desert, known as The Strange Lands. Here, yellow sand stretched on and on as far as the eye could see in every direction. Tall cactuses and jagged rock formations dotted the horizon, and, overhead, a blue sky, streaked with wispy white clouds, threatened to be pulled down by the weight of its impossible size.

A cloth-topped camo Jeep, rolled over the sand; past large, round cactuses with needles as long and as thick as ballpoint pens, a scattering of smooth light-brown rock formations, and a couple of small, scuttling creatures that looked like blue scorpions with human penises for tails instead of stingers.

Conrad was driving the Jeep. Jerry was in the passenger seat and a man named Tom Larson sat in the back of the car with a few dozen crates of guns, explosives, food, water and ammo that would serve both as supplies for the journey, *and* as an offering to the fabled Lucy.

Tom was a friend of Rodman Ryder and a high ranking Company Man within the mercenary division. He was 37-years-old, broad shouldered, square jawed, unshaven and ruddy-faced with small, squinting eyes, bushy eyebrows, and what seemed to be a perpetual scowl.

"The map seems to indicate a large structure five hundred thousand paces east from where we are now," Tom said, staring down at Lucy's map, which was clutched in his hands tightly. Conrad was driving fast, and the paper shook in Tom's hands, threatening to be swept away through one of the open windows.

"Hey, Jerry," Conrad said. "I bet you I can crush that thing over there before it runs away."

Conrad pointed to the thing that he had been referring to, a foot-long, boil-covered rat with six or seven human penises growing out of its back.

"Conrad, leave that thing alone. It's not bothering you," said Jerry.

"C'mon Jerry it's just a rat covered in dicks. I bet I can out run it," said Conrad.

"Can you out run it without running it over?" Jerry asked. "Because I bet you can't."

"Care to make this interesting?" Conrad inquired, wiggling his eyebrows rather obnoxiously.

"Sure. Lets say that if you can't outrun the rat covered in dicks without crushing it, you stop trying to make bets with me about killing things," said Jerry.

"But...what if I *can*?" Conrad asked, attempting to feign innocence, but his smirk betrayed his true intention.

"You can't," said Jerry.

"But what if I *can*?"

"Then you get the satisfaction of knowing that everyone here knows that you can do it," said Jerry.

"Lame," said Conrad.

"You're just saying that because you know you can't do it. Not on foot. Not even in your car even. I mean look at how fast that thing is," Jerry said, pointing to the monstrous rat as it darted along smooth stones, and around blooming cactuses, keeping pace with the moving vehicle. "It's way faster than *you*."

"To fuck it is!" Conrad shouted and a mad grin curled his bristly face as he slammed his foot down on the gas and accelerated.

The rat was a good six or seven car lengths ahead of him and scurrying fast. The needle on the speedometer of Conrad's car rose steadily as the car accelerated. Air poured in through the open windows, sweeping Conrad, Jerry, and Tom's hair backward. Golf ball-sized bugs hit the windshield and were smashed to splatters of puke-green slime.

"Keep going! You're almost past him!" Jerry shouted, grinning. The rat was now only three car lengths in front of Conrad and running straight.

Tom scowled.   He had been traveling with Conrad and Jerry through The Strange Lands for two days. And, though, due to his stoic nature, Tom was not given to displaying emotions of any kind, the two were, in actuality, *driving him insane.*

"Keep going! We're almost there!" Jerry shouted excitedly as the car drew closer to the speeding mutant rat.

"Raaarrr....fuck you, *raaaat*!" Conrad shouted in jest.

Then, the car sped past the rat. The rat, as though sensing it had been defeated, slowed to a stop, and squatted to drop a turd next to a large, round cactus with a translucent pink bloom.

"Yes!" Jerry shouted.

"Yea!" Conrad celebrated.

They high-fived.

"Fuck that rat!" Jerry shouted.

"You know it!" Conrad yelled.

Tom cleared his throat to remind them that he was there.

"The map seems to indicate a large rock formation about 150 paces east," Tom said, and he pointed to a tall rock structure in the distance. "It's to your left."

"Stay on task, *Conrad,*" said Jerry, in a tone of mock sternness. He rolled up a magazine with a picture of a buff blond dude in his underpants on the cover, and bopped Conrad playfully on the back of head with it.

"Yea, yea," Conrad groaned, and he

swerved left, toward the rock formation that Tom had indicated.

As the three men approached the rock formation, its jagged contours became clearer and clearer, until it became apparent that this thing was not a rock formation at all but rather, a large, lopsided, and dented metal cylinder as tall as a skyscraper. The structure was bolted shut around its edges, and the words: "EXPERIMENT 487-B" were printed across its battered surface in stenciled, black, spray paint letters.

"Yup," said Jerry, as he observed the bizarre landmark with an expression that was a mixture of caution, amusement, and awe. "That...that's a thing, *alright!*"

"Dude, fuck that thing. My dick is

bigger," said Conrad.

"Mine too," said Jerry. "Definitely bigger."

It was at this point that Tom found he could contain his bottled rage no longer.

"Alright, *that* is it!" Tom shouted, standing up abruptly. "Both of you, *SHUT UP!*"

Conrad slowed the car and glanced behind him to stare at Tom for a moment.

"Jesus, Tom, what crawled up your ass?" Conrad asked indifferently.

"I am sick of babysitting you two *buffoons!*" Tom shouted, shaking his fists at the sky.

"Relax, dude," said Conrad.

"We're just trying to break up the

ceaseless, unending, unrelenting boredom," said

Jerry grimly. "I mean it's been two days of just

watching a bunch of sand roll by. A man can

only take so much."

In the distance, something screeched a

long, high-pitched *crrraaaaahhhhhhhhhh!*

"You should be glad nothing's attacked

us yet," said Tom.

"No, believe me. I'm glad," said Jerry.

"That doesn't mean driving through The Strange

Lands for two days straight hasn't driven me

nuts."

"Glad. Psh. Speak for yourself. I wanna

kill some shit," growled Conrad.

A green tentacle as tall and as wide as a

subway car burst from the sand to the left of

them, spraying the car with sand, boulders, and shreds of cactus.

"Well, now's your chance, kid," said Tom, regaining his stoic demeanor.

The tentacle rose into the air, and then, slammed itself back down against the sand, creating a truck-sized crater. Conrad accelerated the car, and swerved left to avoid being crushed beneath the slimy, translucent appendage.

"*Crrraaaaaaaaaahhhhhhhhhhgghhhhhhhh!*" the monster shrieked as seven additional tentacles snaked upward from the ground. The sand beneath the car began to tremble, and then, a large, round head the size of a building rose from the sand, lifting the car high into the air. The slimy round head had one large, green eye at the center of it, which opened slowly as sand poured over the monster's face and into piles around it. The monster's mouth was a beak and it opened again to let out another deafening *cccccrrrrraaaaaagggghhhhhhhhhhhhhhhhhh!"*

Tom grabbed a large machine gun and jumped out of the car. Conrad pulled a pistol from his belt with his right hand and a long knife from his belt with his left hand. Then, he burst from the car as well. Jerry jumped in the back of the car and searched the piles of crates frantically for a weapon that could possibly do any damage against a beast so large.

The massive tentacles of the beast shot through the air and it screeched as it attempted, in vain, to knock the three, tiny, itching creatures off of its back. Conrad ran along the monster's slippery green head, weaving to avoid being crushed beneath a downward plummeting tentacle, and then, ducked to avoid a second tentacle, which swung violently towards him, threatening to knock him backward. Tom was a little bit farther along than him, and his gun was raised. He fired at an oncoming tentacle and the monster shrieked again.

"Tom! *Conrad!*" Jerry shouted. "This is a 002 variety beast! Its outer skin is organic but its nerve center is robotic! If you sever the battery it will die!"

"Everybody freaking knows that, *Jerry!*" Conrad shouted back as he slid across the monster's slimy skin toward an oncoming tentacle.   He fired six rounds into the beast, threw his empty gun away, and then, started slicing at it with his sword.

Jerry rifled through the supplies in the back of the car. Then, pulled the top off of one of the larger crates, and found a bundle of explosives. Jerry knelt down, and attempted to lift the bundle of explosives with his knees, but they were very heavy. He stood up, took a deep breath, knelt back down, and attempted to lift the bundle of explosives again.

Tom ran toward an oncoming tentacle, shooting off the contents of his machine gun. The tentacle exploded like an over inflated balloon and clear slime burst from it shriveling translucent skin, drenching Tom's clothes and hair. Tom screamed as his skin began to bubble off of his bloody face. Beneath his scrunched-shut eyelids a pair of blind, searing eyes melted into jelly. The monster swatted him off of its back with another tentacle, and his body flew through the air, and off into the distance, disappearing from sight.

Seeing what the corrosive life-blood of the beast had done to Tom, Conrad lowered his sword and began running. He knew that the monster's nerve center; its battery, had to be somewhere. But where? 002 variety beasts with tentacles usually had a battery on one of the tips of its tentacles that could be severed to disable the beast in the event of a rampage. However, which tentacle the battery was located in could only be known by whoever had built the thing, and slicing the wrong tentacle, it seemed, could mean being burned to a bloody eye-less cadaver.

Jerry emerged from the car, carrying a small crate. He ran toward Conrad.

"Conrad!" he shouted.

A tentacle swooped down and knocked Jerry's feet out from under him. He fell backwards and the crate slipped out of his hands.

"Jerry!" Conrad shouted back, running towards him.

Another tentacle hurtled forward and punched Jerry in the stomach. It knocked him backward and, this time, he stayed down.

"Get the box, Conrad! It's Zebbic!" Jerry

shouted and the tentacle wrapped itself around his head, obstructing his nose and mouth. His body flailed and he gasped for breath.

"Jerry!" Conrad shouted again. He didn't dare slice the monster's tentacle off of Jerry for fear that its acidic lifeblood would melt the man's face off.

Conrad grabbed the box that Jerry had dropped, ripped the top off of it, and found a syringe. It must have been filled with the substance toxic to Strange Lands beasts known as Zebbic. A thick purple liquid sloshed around inside the tube of the hypodermic needle as Conrad ran with it. Zebbic, in this extremely rare and ultra-concentrated form, was very expensive and difficult to manufacture. He would have to put this stuff to good use. Because there probably wasn't much more of it, hidden in the car.

Conrad plunged his sword downward into the monster's head and twisted it. Clear liquid squirted upward, scorching splatters of holes in the calves of his jeans.

"Cccraaaaaaahhhhhhh!" the monster shrieked. Then, its massive eye shifted upward. Conrad felt the eye's gooey surface slide beneath his feet as the monster's round body rolled in the sand. Its beak-like mouth, just below the eye, opened wide, and a forked tongue the size of a subway car emerged, with the intension of slurping Conrad into its gaping beak and devouring him whole. Conrad stabbed the approaching tongue with the hypodermic needle, and, compressed the plunger, injecting the beast with the thick, purple liquid contained within.

The monster shrieked its final shriek. Then, it shriveled slightly, its translucent green body becoming contaminated by a growing cloud of murky purple. Its massive eyelids closed with a deafening *crash!* Its tentacles shriveled into tight coils and it collapsed into the sand, at long last, *dead*.

2

"Jerry....*Jerry!*"

Jerry who lay face up and spread-eagle in the sand, opened his eyes slowly. He saw Conrad standing over him, looking concerned but also excited. The glare of the scorching sun overhead made the edges of his blond hair glow like the halo of a celestial being.

"Ughh....*Conrad*?" Jerry murmured back. "Where's the monster?....Where's Tom?"

"Yea. I killed the monster," Conrad informed Jerry proudly. "You must have hit your head when the thing rolled over to try and eat me because you've been out cold for like three hours."

Jerry sat up and brushed the sand out of his disheveled hair.

"And Tom?" he asked.

"Also dead," Conrad informed him bluntly. "The monster bled acid on him and burned his eyes and all of his skin off."

"Jesus," Jerry commented. A gruesome image of flesh melting off of the bones of a screaming man invaded his mind.

"Oh well," said Conrad, shrugging. "He died in the line of duty, like we probably all will eventually."

"He died so that we could exterminate that abomination, Strange Lands Lucy," said Jerry grimly, and then, he stood up. "It was an honorable death."

"Yea, I guess it was," sighed Conrad.

"We'll kill her for him, Conrad," said Jerry grimly. "So that he didn't die in vain."

"You said it," said Conrad. "That bastard is as good as dead."

"She doesn't stand a chance."

Jerry glanced around him and saw the massive carcass of the purple-splotched green beast drying in the sun, like a beached jellyfish the size of a mountain. In every other direction he looked, there was nothing but sand.

"Where's the car?" Jerry asked morosely.

"It's underneath of the monster, I think," said Conrad.

"*Fuck.*"

"You said it."

"Where's the map?" Jerry asked.

Conrad dug his hand into his back pocket and pulled out a crumpled piece of paper. Then, he pulled the piece of paper open and smoothed it flat with his hand.

"I managed to save it," Conrad said.

Jerry sighed.

"Well, at least we have *that*," he said. "Hey, Conrad?"

"Yea?"

Jerry took the map out of Conrad's hands, examined it for a moment, and then, began walking. Conrad followed.

"Who do you think built the Strange Lands beasts?" Jerry asked.

"Huh?"

"I mean, some of them are mechanical. The thing we just killed was probably some kind of cyborg hybrid. And that means that someone has to be building them....or that someone has sort of just built them...and then stopped," said Jerry.

"Hm...I never really thought about it before. I guess you must be right...," Conrad murmured pensively.

"But who built them...and *why*?" Jerry asked. He kept walking, pulled back his sleeve, glanced at a compass in his large wrist watch, and then, changed direction. Conrad followed him.

"I don't know. The Overlords probably," said Conrad. "*Why* is probably the better question."

Jerry walked past a few small, round cactuses covered in pink blooms. A sand-colored snake with a human arm for a tail twisted sideways through the sand, and then, dug its way headfirst underground.

"I mean, when you think about it....," Jerry mused. "Why is any of this stuff here?"

"I don't know. Why are *we* here? Is there a God? Did we just kind of show up out of no where? There's really no way to know for sure," said Conrad. He yawned and stretched as he walked behind Jerry, then, plucked a few pink blossoms off of a tall cactus as he strolled by it. The letter attached to Lucy's map had said that Lucy would accept flowers as an offering, and now that the car was buried underneath of that monster, he had nothing else to offer her but the weapons he carried on his person. It was a meager offering and adding the flowers to it was really and act of desperation on his part.

"Does it ever drive you crazy not to

know?" Jerry asked. He kept walking and Conrad followed, every so often, picking another cactus flower to add to his bouquet for Lucy. Sure his offering was going to be a little light on the practical supplies, but it was in Conrad's nature to be optimistic and he couldn't help but imagine that if he put enough effort into the flower arrangement, Lucy might feel bad for him and have sex with him anyway. Of course it was stupid to assume that the bloody-crotched she-beast of legend had emotions. It was more likely that, like the shmale infants before their heads and limbs were circumcised, she lacked the capacity to feel anything. However, if there was a fraction of a percent of a chance that Lucy would be impressed enough by these flowers to have sex with him, Conrad was going to try it.

"Conrad?" Jerry said to get Conrad's attention.

"Huh?"

"Does it ever drive you crazy not to know?" Jerry asked again.

"I guess...I try not to think about it," said Conrad.

"Yea, me too," admitted Jerry. "But sometimes, you know, you just can't help it. Where did this stuff come from? Why is it here? I mean, did *God* put it here? Are The Overlords God? Who are The Overlords even?"

"I like to think that they're like Santa Claus," said Conrad.

Jerry laughed.

"You know like they buy you cool shit once a year, and then, the rest of the year they just fuck off and leave you alone," Conrad continued.

"Is that what the connection is?" said Jerry, grinning.

"Psh. The fuck if I know what the connection is! For all I know The Overlords are like the Easter Bunny because they shit eggs made of chocolate wrapped in gold foil!"

"Or...The Overlords are like the Easter Bunny because they're a story that we're told and we believe it because that's what's expected of us," said Jerry. "I've always thought that The Overlords might have been a rumor started by The Company so that it could deny responsibility for unpopular policies....you know, blame it on a higher power. A higher power that won't see reason, and has the ability and the desire to blow our whole society straight to shit," said Jerry.

"Interesting theory," said Conrad. "But I'd keep it to myself if I were you. I don't imagine The Company would like people walking around with ideas like that."

"I don't imagine they would," said Jerry. "Just don't tell anyone I said that, ok?"

Conrad mimed zipping his mouth closed and throwing away a key.

"Hey man, there's nothing out here to witness your treasonous talk but a bunch of sand and mindless monsters," said Conrad. "Your secret's safe."

"How did it get to the point where we're even afraid to talk about things like this?" Jerry mused darkly.

"Security cameras. Company surveillance. Dirty looks," Conrad answered bluntly as though the answer were obvious, which of course, it was.

"Yea," Jerry confirmed. "That sounds about right."

The sun sank low in the sky, bathing the horizon in waves of purple and orange. In the distance, an unseen monster let out a loud, rattling noise that was halfway between a serpent's hiss and a lion's roar.

"The sun's going down," Conrad said.

"We're almost there," said Jerry. "Let's keep going."

"Alright."

The two were silent for awhile as they walked. Jerry peered down at the map periodically, and then, checked his compass to see that they were still going in the right direction. The sun sank lower. The sky grew darker. Creatures hidden by the growing darkness cawed and clicked and chirped and creaked.

"There it is," Jerry said after awhile.

Conrad looked up and saw that Jerry was pointing to a wooden sign a few dozen feet away. The sign was crooked and its post was half-buried in the sand. The two men walked up to it. Two words were spray painted on the sign in pink cursive letters: *Welcome Suitors.*"

Jerry walked closer to the sign, brushed some sand off of it, and shrugged.

"Well...the map says that The Cult of Lucy is here," said Jerry.

"Maybe they only come out during the day," Conrad proposed.

"I don't understand. Is this whole thing just some kind of a prank? Maybe there is no Lucy," said Jerry, sounding distressed.

Conrad walked up to the sign. They both stared at it sullenly for a moment, and then, the weight of their combined bodies made the trap door underneath of them fall open. Both men screamed as they felt the ground disappear beneath them and they plummeted feet-first into the dark depths of the hazardous and terrifying unknown.

3

The trap door opened into a metal cylinder, which stretched down several dozen feet beneath the surface of the sand. The cylinder, in turn, opened into a large cage, the floor of which, was covered in straw.

A man in a green and brown splotched camouflage jumpsuit, holding a long-barreled rifle with both hands, turned in the direction of the cage as he heard Conrad and Jerry's bodies hit the ground. The man's hair was close-cut and brown and his face was young, but bristly and darkly tanned.

"Brother Vince." the man in the camouflage jump shut announced deeply, speaking into a blue tooth cell phone ear piece. The blue LED light on the thing flashed a few times as he was speaking. "We have *'suitors'*."

Jerry and Conrad stood up, brushed strands of hay off of their clothes, and glanced around, observing that they were in a cage and that the cage was inside of a dimly lit underground tunnel. The tunnel had rough, dirt walls speckled with small, flat stones. Clusters of white cactus roots dangled from its arched ceiling.

Ten or twenty men wearing baggy camouflage pants, white sleeveless shirts with or with out camouflage jackets, and large brown or black boots, appeared at the end of the tunnel, and walked up to the cage where Jerry and Conrad stood. The men were all young, muscular, and tan with close cut hair and serious expressions. They each carried a rifle either strapped to their back or clutched in both hands as though prepared to fire at them.

The group of camouflage-clad men stood for a moment, and then, backed against the walls of the tunnel, parting so that there was a clear path between them.

A tall, curvy woman with pale skin and blond hair was made visible. She wore a short, hot-pink, sleeveless dress with white high heals and a lacy pink and white ribbon around her neck. The woman walked over to the cage where Conrad and Jerry stood, and, as she moved, the tunnel was silent. Her sharp white heals clinked against the stone floor of the tunnel and she smirked sinisterly. A man with a buzz cut, wearing a camouflage bandana walked behind her, and beside her, walked a large grey Irish wolfhound.

Conrad walked to the edge of the cage, and stood as close to this woman as it was possible to stand without pressing his face stupidly against the bars. Upon closer inspection he saw that she had long, wavy, sunflower yellow hair, and her full lips were painted red. Her large blue eyes were outlined in black paint and the lids were tinted a pale blue.

"I...I can't believe it's you," Conrad whispered, as much to himself as to the woman. He was not exactly sure if she could talk or even if she was smart enough to understand English. Yet, for a moment, he still expected her to answer.

She did not answer, however. She merely stared at him through black-ringed eyes with a hungry, animal expression. There was something of malice about her, a sort of unspoken sadism that tainted the contours of her beautiful face.

"We are The Cult of Lucy!" the man with the camouflage bandana announced for Jerry and Conrad's benefit. "My name is Brother Vince." He motioned toward the smirking woman, whose large, blue eyes were glued to Conrad like he was a piece of fresh, bloody, dripping meat and she was a starving animal. "And this is Lucy."

Lucy crouched down and whispered something in Brother Vince's ear, covering her mouth with her hand as she did so. Then, she withdrew her hand and straightened up again, her expression, unchanged.

"Lucy wants to know if you've come to kill her," Brother Vince informed them.

"No. Of course not." Conrad lied. "We're here to join The Cult of Lucy."

Lucy crouched down again, lifted her hand over her mouth and whispered something else in Brother Vince's ear. Then, after some time, straightened up and began staring creepily into Conrad's eyes.

"Lucy says that she has killed many, many men in the desert, a number of them Company Men tasked with her extermination....and all of them, at first, claimed to be her admirers. Lucy requests that you present your offering as a token of your true intent," Brother Vince said.

"And why can't Lucy tell us this *herself?*" Jerry asked angrily, narrowing his eyes with distain.

"Lucy is a creature called a shman, or a woman, if you prefer. Her voice is shriller and more high pitched than the voice of any man that you have ever heard. It has been known to cause extreme pain and damage the eardrums. Those who are not accustomed to it, sometimes experience total hearing loss," Brother Vince explained.

"*Bullshit,*" Jerry accused bluntly, and he pointed in Brother Vince's direction. "I know bullshit when I hear it and that's *bullshit.*"

Brother Vince became visibly angry upon hearing this.

"I translate for her as a courtesy to you, so that you do not go permanently deaf!" Brother Vince shouted indignantly and Lucy nodded in agreement, smirking as she did so.

"Woah, *woah.* Hey, man! We don't want to go deaf, ok?" Conrad said quickly, putting up his hands in supplication. "We have an offering for Lucy. We had more but it got destroyed by Strange Lands beasts on the way here."

"A convenient excuse," said Brother Vince humorlessly. "Present your offering before Lucy or die."

"Um…ok," Conrad said. He removed the long knife from his belt and set it down on the floor in front of him. Then, he removed a pair of pistols from the belt, a grenade, a pair of nun chucks, a ninja throwing star, a pair of handcuffs, and an electric taser. He put each of these things down on the ground in front of him. Then, he put the bundle of pink cactus flowers, he had collected while walking through the desert, down, on top of the pile of weapons.

"It's not much," said Conrad, "But it's all

I've got. I hope that it will aid the Followers of Lucy in their noble cause."

Lucy crouched down and whispered something in Brother Vince's ear.

"Lucy says your offering *sucks*," Brother Vince informed them bluntly. "She says that she will kill both of you if you cannot produce a better offering."

The men surrounding Lucy raised their rifles and aimed them at Jerry and Conrad's heads and torsos.

"Jerry," Conrad murmured, nudging Jerry with his shoulder.

"Right," said Jerry. He searched his pockets frantically for things that he could offer to Lucy in exchange for their lives.

Jerry found a paper clip, a pencil eraser, and a few pennies in the pockets of his slacks. He put these things down next to Conrad's offering. Then, he unhooked his gun from his belt and put it down on the pile. He glanced over at Lucy, whose smirk had now been usurped by a hateful scowl. Then, he hastily removed his dark blue tie and threw that on the pile as well.

Lucy whispered something in Brother Vince's ear.

"Lucy says that your offering is an insult and that you must die," said Brother Vince.

The men surrounding Lucy released the safeties on their aimed rifles with a unanimous *click*.

"Wait, *wait*, we have more!" Jerry said quickly. "What Conrad said is true. We had more but we lost it when we were attacked by a Strange Lands beast."

"It's true," said Conrad, "We brought a bigger offering than this...It's still there under the 002 beast."

"*Prove it*," Brother Vince growled. He removed his own rifle from the holster on his back and aimed it at Conrad's head.

"It's still there," said Conrad. "The car, I mean...it's wrecked but it's full of weapons, ammunition and food and water that was supposed to be an offering to Lucy. We couldn't take it with us after the car was wrecked. There's too much of it."

"Very well," said Brother Vince, lowering his gun. "You lead us too it. We'll spare your life."

Lucy's scowl curled into the smirk again. She crouched down and whispered something into Brother Vince's ear, then, straightened back up again and winked.

"And you will be allowed a private session with Lucy," said Brother Vince. "By which I mean, *sex*. Incase that wasn't clear."

"Then, Brother Vince," said Conrad, grinning. A private sexual encounter with Lucy was really the ideal situation. That way, without any resistance, he could satisfy his sexual curiosity about her before easily snapping her delicate neck in his hands. "We will get Lucy that offering."

4

That night, Conrad and Jerry slept in the cage. Though the hay, which lined the cage, was softer and more comfortable than the metal floor of the cage, it was still not very soft or very comfortable and they did not sleep well. They did not, however, discuss their plans to kill Lucy, for fear that they would be overheard, or that the cage was bugged with cameras or recording devices.

In the morning, the brothers of the cult of Lucy woke them, briefly patted them down for weapons, and then, tied their hands behind their backs. Conrad complained about this but did not resist. His best chance to have his shot at

Lucy was to get these men to trust him and resistance to measures put in place to protect Lucy might have tipped them off.

"There's no need to restrain us. We would never hurt Lucy. I mean, if we really wanted to hurt Lucy, don't you think we would have tried it by now?" Conrad said to the men as they were tying his hands behind his back.

A man that he recognized as Arnold Copperfield (from the company file photos) replied:

"It's more likely that you plan to kill Lucy and then escape with your lives to reap the reward. If you had shot her in the tunnel, our brothers would have shot you dead. And then, even, if by some miracle, you had managed to gun us all down...well then, you would have just starved to death in that cage. No. I think you're waiting for a better opportunity."

"Yea, man, don't worry about this. We all had to go through this at some point," said a different man in a camouflage jump suit. He spoke in a much more friendly tone than Arnold, as he tied Jerry's hands behind his back. "But it is a necessary precaution. Believe it or not, there are a lot of psychos out there who would love to slice Lucy's head off. Yea, so don't worry, man. We'll untie you after you've earned Lucy trust with your offering. I'm Brother Tony, by the way."

5

Ten or so members of the cult of Lucy

piled into the back of an open-topped, mud green military car. Arnold Copperfield (now "Brother Arnold") and the man in the jumpsuit, who called himself "Brother Tony" walked on either side of Conrad and Jerry with their rifles aimed at the sides of their heads. They led them into a second open-topped military car, this one painted with green and brown splotched camouflage.

Lucy sat in the passenger seat of this car, next to Brother Vince, who was in the driver's seat. Today, Lucy was wearing a slightly longer powder pink dress with glittery pink heals and a translucent pink frill. There was a translucent pink ribbon tied around her neck and a few pink cactus flowers woven into the braids of her sunflower yellow hair. In her left hand, she carried a pink camisole with a white handle and Japanese cherry blossoms painted over its fabric portions. Her right hand clutched the bouquet of flowers that Conrad had given her. She buried her face in the bouquet every so often and closed her eyes. The Irish wolf hound sat between her and Brother Vince, quiet, still, and attentive. The dog was tense and his teeth were bared as though ready to strike.

Brother Arnold and Brother Tony led Conrad and Jerry to the back of the car. They got in and Brother Vince began driving. The mud green car followed.

"The monster is four or five hours west from here," Jerry informed Brother Vince.

Brother Vince nodded and revved the engine of the vehicle as he sped forward into the seemingly endless sand.

"It better be," Brother Vince growled.

Lucy turned back toward them for a moment, winked, and blew Jerry a kiss. The gesture took Jerry by surprise so that he was unable to repress a reflexive shutter. There was something very unwholesome about that look on her face. It was unsettling.

The cars drove through yellow sand, past tall cactuses, jutting rock formations, and a couple of hopping toads with extra limbs and too many eyes. A scorpion with a human finger for a tail instead of a stinger emerged from a burrow in the sand, and caught a scurrying, two-headed rat in its pincers, *then* withdrew back into its burrow, pulling the rat down with it.

After some time, the brothers of The Cult of Lucy reached the massive green beast that Conrad had slain. By now, the monster had deflated considerably. Its once gelatinous exo-skin was shriveled and dry and now, the entire thing resembled a massive raisin beneath a relentless sun. It must have started rotting already because it stunk like death.

"Ok, so where's the offering?" Brother Vince demanded impatiently. He removed the bandana from his head and tied it over his nose and mouth to filter out the stench of rot.

"Um...," Conrad mumbled nervously. "The thing is...I'm not really sure where it landed. It might actually be….underneath of the monster."

"Underneath of the monster?" Brother Vince repeated angrily. "That fucking thing is as big as a mountain!"

"A hill maybe," said Jerry to nobody in particular.

"*Fuck you,*" Brother Vince spat at Jerry and he turned backward to point at him and glare venomously.

Lucy put the bouquet of flowers down on the dashboard and got out of the car. She removed her heals and carried them in her free hand as she walked barefoot in the sand, toward the giant, rotting monster.

Brother Vince got out of the car and ran

after her.

"Lucy, *sweetheart*, where are you going?" Brother Vince called half lovingly, half patronizingly.

Lucy did not respond or turn to acknowledge him. She kept walking.

The other brothers of The Cult of Lucy got out of their cars and began following her. Brother Arnold and Brother Tony stood up as well.

"Let's go," Brother Tony said to Conrad and Jerry and he nudged Jerry's shoulder gently with his hand.

Brother Arnold bopped Conrad on the head with the barrel of his rifle.

"*Ow*," Conrad complained, glaring

hatefully at Brother Arnold as he stood up.

"Come on," Brother Arnold grunted.

Conrad and Jerry walked along with the rest of the brothers of the Cult of Lucy. Brother Arnold and Brother Tony walked behind with their rifles pressed to the back of their captive's heads.

Lucy knelt down in the sand in front of the monster. She reached into her shirt and withdrew a long knife from between her breasts. Conrad recognized the knife as his own and felt a strange sense of pride as he watched her unsheave it and plunge its gleaming tip into the carcass of the monster. Lucy pulled the knife through the skin of the beast, sawing a small square in its withered green skin. Then, she pulled the square of skin free and laid it down in the sand, next to where she was kneeling. The robotic inner shell of the monster was left bare and appeared as a curved sheet of silver metal with a few rivets in it. Lucy knocked on the metal surface with one long, slender hand, and Conrad noticed for the first time that she was wearing a pair of white lace fingerless gloves. Her fingernails were long and sharp like an animal's and they were painted a bright shade of glossy bubblegum pink.

"Somebody get a blowtorch!" Brother Vince instructed.

A couple of brothers ran back to the mud green car and retrieved a large blow torch, which they handed off to Brother Vince.

"Back away, dear," said Brother Vince to Lucy and she rose to her feet, taking several steps backward.

Brother Vince raised the blow torch and started burning through the dead monster's organic exo-skin and metal inner chamber. After an hour or so, he was able to scorch an opening in the beast's corpse large enough for a man to step through. It seemed that the monster was hollow and that its insides were vast and dark.

"I need a flashlight!" Brother Vince demanded.

A man ran back to the camouflage-painted vehicle and returned with a large flashlight. Brother Vince took the flashlight out of the man's hands and clicked it on. Then, he stepped into the body of the rotting monster. He fumbled around in the dark for a moment. Then, he spotted a light switch on the wall, which he flicked on. Rows of fluorescent lights built into the ceiling lit up, revealing an empty metal room.

"Guys, you better get in here and see this!" Brother Vince called to the rest of them.

The brothers of The Cult of Lucy filtered into the room one at a time. They observed it with expressions ranging from disbelief to a kind of inspired awe, which suggested they were having a religious experience. Brother Vince walked to the door at the edge of the room. It was made of metal and there was a circular metal crank at the center of it, the kind that is built into a bank vault. Brother Vince crouched down and seized the crank in both hands. Then, he turned it slowly counter clock wise. The door creaked open and he stepped through it.

"My god. There's a building inside this monster," he announced as much to himself as to the men who accompanied him. He walked out into a metal hallway lined with doors, and then, stared upward into an impossibly high, arched ceiling lined with fluorescent lights.

"Jesus...this thing could be one hell of a mansion," said one of the brothers.

"...Or an apartment complex...," said another of the brothers.

Lucy walked over to Brother Vince, lifted

her hand over her mouth, and whispered something in his ear. Brother Vince pulled away from her and turned in the direction of Conrad and Jerry, who were still being dragged along at gun point.

"Lucy humbly accepts your offering," Brother Vince informed them. "And has granted your request to join us as a brother in The Cult of Lucy."

"Sweet," said Conrad. "Are you going to untie us now?"

Lucy put her hand over her mouth and whispered something in Brother Vince's ear. Then, backed away, and nodded, grinning.

"Lucy will reward your grand offering by sharing with one of you, the gift of her body," said Brother Vince.

"Great!" said Conrad, grinning, and he stepped forward, rolling his shoulders, which ached from being pulled backward by the force of his bonds. Lucy smirked at him mischievously as his face drew close to hers and Conrad drew his tongue along the contours of his large, white teeth hungrily. "Let's get this party started."

"Not so fast there, slick," said Brother Vince, grabbing Conrad by one of his muscular shoulders and pulling him away from Lucy. "Lucy likes your friend."

"...Huh?" Conrad murmured, confused.

Two brothers untied Jerry and he stumbled forward, for a moment, looking terrified. He straightened up, smoothed back his hair, and all of the emotion faded from his face.

Lucy walked down the hallway and into one of the many doorways, which lined its metal surface. Jerry followed slowly, shuffling his feet as he went. His hands were shaking, but his face was still blank; expressionless. He moved like a doll in the hands of a child with a porcelain face and straight wooden legs.

Then, Lucy popped out of the room and grabbed him by the front of his shirt, pulling him inside. The sharp noise of the metal door slamming shut behind them made Conrad flinch. There was a good chance that Lucy would not emerge from that room alive.

6

Jerry took a deep breath and glanced around the room. It was a long, box shaped-room with silver walls and rows of fluorescent lights built into the ceiling. There was nothing in the room except for a thick layer of dust on the floor and the still smirking Lucy. She stared at him with large blue eyes and licked her lips. Jerry stared back and said nothing. This was the perfect opportunity to kill her. After all, they were alone. No cult members would step in to defend her and there was no place to run in this room. No furniture, or large objects, that the she-beast could use in her defense, as bludgeons. Legend had it that shmen where significantly weaker than men. Jerry had no weapons with him, other than his own fists but, perhaps, that was all it would take. Perhaps, this would be easy.

Lucy walked over to him slowly, and ceased the fly of his pants. She stared into his eyes, as she did this, and then, began to pull the zipper down. Jerry pushed her off of him and she stumbled backward, taken by surprise. The smirk on her face flickered for a moment, but then, returned. She licked her lips again and rubbed her pink satin clad breasts with the palms of her hands. Jerry shuttered and took a step forward, his hands tightening into fists; his eyebrows drawing together with rage.

"I don't understand how anyone could like something as repulsive as you. You're not even a man…you're just some kind of an animal, *like a chimpanzee* or some kind of a mindless parasite; except you're worse than that, aren't you? You're a monster, a *disgusting*, hideous abomination," raved Jerry hatefully, putting up his fists "And its time for you to die."

Jerry ran forward and punched Lucy in the face. Lucy stumbled backward, and her mad grin broadened slowly, her large, blue eyes glued to the glare of Jerry's thick glasses. Then, she began to laugh. Her voice was at least two octaves deeper than Conrad's. Perhaps it was even an octave deeper than the voice of the buff black actor who played Testosterone Tyrone.

"I'm going to mop the floor with you, you little pre-school piece of shit," Lucy boomed between fits of hysterical laughter, and then, she swung her fist and hit Jerry in the face. His body flew backward and the back of his head hit one of the metal walls with a metallic *clunk*.

Jerry stood up quickly; his head spinning; his mouth dripping with blood. He spit a nasty mixture of red saliva and broken teeth out onto the floor, and then, wiped more blood off of his face and broken nose with the back of his hand.

Lucy laughed, and then, charged toward him again, her fists raised. Jerry dodged a second punch aimed at his head and lunged for Lucy's throat. There was a piece of cartilage at the top of the human neck, which, when crushed, resulted in death. Jerry's index finger and thumb closed around it, then Lucy pulled away and kicked him in the stomach.

"Ugh!" he shouted, reflexively bending forward and clutching his stomach. Lucy cackled and slammed her fist into his nose, snapping it sideways, blood poured from both of his nostrils and over the lower half of his cringing face as he was knocked backward. Then, Lucy hit him in the face, with her other fist, between the eyes, blackening them both shut. Jerry fell backward onto the floor and Lucy cackled as she kicked him in the face, snapping his already snapped left nose so that it snapped right with a nauseating *crunch*.

Jerry stood slowly, squinting through swollen purple eyes. The world was spinning around him, his stomach was turning with nausea. He lunged forward a second time, aiming for Lucy's throat. Lucy laughed, and grabbed Jerry by the throat, easily pushing him away, then, her fingers tightened and she began strangling him. Jerry choked and gasped as his air supply was cut off from the neck. He felt the blood rush to his head and his eyes bulge as he gasped for air. Lucy was a lot taller than him and she stared down into his cracked and crooked glasses, smirking as she lifted him into the air by his throat. He choked and his feet kicked in the air as his hands flew to Lucy's hands and grabbed at them, desperately attempting to pry them off of his neck. Lucy laughed and laughed and laughed. Lights popped in Jerry's eyes and he went limp in her hands. Then, she dropped him like a sack of lank shit and he fell in a pile on the floor at her feet.

<u>7</u>

Lucy dragged Jerry out of the room by the back of his shirt and tossed his bloody body so that if fell face down on the floor next to where Conrad stood.

"You fucking piece of shit!" Conrad boomed, storming toward Lucy with his fists raised. Five or six cult brothers jumped on him and held him back.

Lucy gave Conrad the finger, and readjusted the large pink ribbon, which was slipping down her neck, briefly revealing a large Adam's apple. The dog bounded over to her and stood by her side, tense, teeth bared; prepared to lunge.

"Fuck you, Conrad! Your stupid friend tried to kill me!" Lucy boomed back.

Her voice was uncommonly deep. And it was a voice that Conrad recognized instantly.

"Fuck...*Wyatt?* Is that *you*?" Conrad replied, nonplused.

"My name," said Lucy, walking up the Conrad with her (his?) hands on his hips. He put his index finger on Conrad's forehead and tapped him roughly. "Is *Lucy*."

"So you're not a shman at all?" Conrad growled with both frustration and disappointment.

"No, but I'm as close as you're going to

get," said Lucy, "And I prefer she/her pronouns if you don't mind, Conrad."

"...But does that mean that...you don't really have a...a...*incubation chamber*?" Conrad stuttered in confusion.

The brothers of The Cult of Lucy all broke out into a fit of hysterical laughter.

"No, dip shit, live shmen that walk around and talk and stuff aren't real," growled Lucy, "The biological ones are just empty husks that were born without brain cavities."

"So you're just a decoy," growled Conrad. "Where are you hiding the real Strange Lands Lucy?"

"Strange Lands Lucy's not real, you stupid fucker," Lucy said. "That's just a scam we use to lure people out here so we can kill them and steal their shit."

"What? This doesn't even make sense. Didn't death eye kill you?" Conrad murmured.

"I survived in the monster's belly, and then, cut myself out after it had wandered far into The Strange Lands," Lucy bragged. "Because in my heart, I think...I always wanted to live as Lucy. Her legend spoke to me...and ever since I was a little boy, I knew...that I was destined to become her. And the only way to do that, Conrad, to live as Lucy, just as I have always dreamed, was to fuck around with the Manazonian government...and I've done that. I've done that in spades. When word got out that there was a live shman wandering around the desert, collecting followers, the government just had to send Company Men after me. They like to keep it quiet but the truth is."

Lucy grinned evilly: "I've killed so many that I've lost count. I even started leaving clues so that more confused hetero saps come and bring me more offerings, by which, of course, I mean: money and cool shit."

Lucy walked over to Brother Vince and cradled his bristly faced lovingly in her long, elegant hand.

"Though a few were so regaled by my womanly charms that they opted instead to join my cult," she continued. "It's a shame, Conrad. There was a time in my life when I really did love you...in a way. I really did hope that you would join us."

"No, Wyatt, I won't join you," Conrad muttered angrily, and he struggled to free himself from the five or six men that were holding him back, so that two more men felt the need to rush over, and clock him on the head with the barrels of their guns. A trickle of blood spilled down over his forehead and he dropped to his knees.

Conrad lowered his head so that his deep-set eyes were masked in shadow.

"After what you did to Jerry, I'll see to it that you all die," he growled.

Lucy walked up to him and backhanded him across the face, so that his head was forced sideways with a sharp *slap*.

"Wrong answer, you ignorant, arrogant *fuck*," Lucy growled. "I was going to forgive your transgressions against me, and make you my right hand man. But as much as I'd like to trust you, Conrad...I don't think that it would be wise. No...it seems...you've sided with The Company and with the oppressive Manazonian gorilla state, which seeks to rob me of my right to free self expression. So...now you get to die in the desert with this piece-of-shit government stooge you're so fond of."

Lucy pointed to Jerry who was bloody and crumpled but as far as Conrad could tell, still breathing. Conrad blinked back tears.

"If you hurt him, I'll kill you! Do you understand? I'll make you sorry you ever touched him!" Conrad screamed, attempting to lunge at Lucy again. A wall of cult brothers got between him and Lucy.

"That hurts my feelings, Conrad. After all that we've been through, you'd really come to *his* defense instead of *mine*? You'd really throw your lot in with some asshole that tried to kill me? After *he* struck *me...first*?" said Lucy with a dangerous, forced grin, "I'm disappointed, Conrad....I really thought that you, of all people, *would understand.*"

8

The brothers of the cult of Lucy tossed Conrad over the back of the mud green military car and his large body landed in the yellow sand with a loud *thud*. The smoldering sun overhead beat down on his cringing face and sweat pricked his forehead, causing his short blond bangs to stick to his skin. Conrad heard a second, softer thud that must have been Lucy's men chucking Jerry out of the car as well. Conrad struggled to move his arms and legs but they had been bound tightly with rope. He sat up abruptly and glared into Lucy's large blue eyes. Lucy smirked back and sashayed to the back of the car, so that her long shadow fell over the glowering Conrad.

"I suppose you're wondering why I chose to model my alter ego after the legend of Strange Lands Lucy," Lucy said, and then, she paused as though waiting for verbal confirmation of her assumption.

Conrad continued to glare at Lucy and did not reply.

Lucy continued: "It's because Strange Lands Lucy is *free*, Conrad. She does not think. She does not feel. She does not imagine. She does not create. She does not love. She is completely free."

Lucy paused dramatically as she pulled one of the pink cactus flowers out of a braid in her hair and twirled it in her slender, elegant hand.

"When I am Lucy," Lucy said, staring down into Conrad's squinting cobalt blue eyes. "I feel no pain. I am as indifferent to your suffering as this flower."

Lucy released the cactus flower and it

drifted downward slowly, landing a few inches above the soles of Conrad's boots in the sand.

"Rest in peace, my old friend," Lucy said with a somberness that was only half ironic. Then, she hitched up her skirt and pulled a gun out of a holster strapped to her thigh. She pointed the gun at Conrad and Conrad stared back, resolute, unflinching, ready to die with dignity. Lucy smirked and she moved her hand slowly to the left so that the gun was pointed at Jerry. Her grin broadened, and then, she pulled the trigger and shot Jerry in the chest.

"*Jerry!*" Conrad yelled as he watched an explosion of crimson liquid erupt from Jerry's chest. Jerry's mouth fell open slowly and he collapsed backwards onto the sand.

Then, Lucy shouted a cheerful: "Let's ride, boys!"

The brothers of The Cult of Lucy cheered and a few of them hooted and high-fived as the car sped off into the distance. The dog bounded up and down the length of the car howling as though to join in.

Conrad watched them disappear with a look of hatred that twisted his handsome face. Wyatt had made a fool out of him. He had made a fool out of the entire Company. There was no Strange Lands Lucy and there was no intact shman walking around outside of its tube. It was all just a trick to lure Company Men out to The Strange Lands and steal their weapons.

Conrad felt sad in a way that he had not

felt sad in a very long time.   He collapsed backward into the sand and turned his head toward Jerry, whose bloody chest was heaving rapidly.

"...*Jerry*...," he murmured weakly.   The sweltering heat from the sun overhead was already starting to make him feel disoriented.

"...*What*?" Jerry murmured back bitterly between heavy, pain-wracked breaths.

"I...*I*....," Conrad whispered, his voice quivering slightly.   Throughout his lifetime, he had been trained and conditioned to never cry, yet, at this moment, he felt very close to tears. He fell silent again for fear that if he spoke another word he would loose control and break into a spasm of shameful sniveling.   *No*.   If he was going to die. He was going to do it with dignity.

Conrad closed his eyes slowly, and the last thing he saw before he shut them completely. Was Jerry's face: stone cold and emotionless; bound hands powerless to press against his seeping chest wound.

Conrad was relieved to escape to a dark quiet place behind his eyelids where he would not have to watch such a thing.

<u>9</u>

At the age of twenty, Both of Tom's arms had been blown off after a failed attempt to defuse a bomb in The Company training school. The Company had provided him with a pair of robotic arms to replace them and, after a few months, his skin had grown right over the prosthetics and down to the tips of his fingers, concealing the mechanics underneath and giving him the appearance of a normal man. At the age of twenty-three, Tom had been shot multiple times during a dispute with a prominent Manazonian gang. His kneecaps had been shattered, his spine severed, and the meat in his organs, chest, stomach, and legs filled with as many wholes as a block of Swiss cheese. Consequentially, The Manazonian government provided him with a series of reconstructive surgeries, during which, his organic spine was replaced by a robotic one, his torso and most of the organs contained with in it were replaced by a series of roughly equivalent mechanical substitutes. His kneecaps had been shattered, his spine severed, and the meat in his organs, chest, stomach and legs filled with as many wholes as a block of Swiss cheese. Consequentially, The Manazonian government provided him with a series of reconstructive surgeries, during which his organic spine was replace by a robotic one, his torso and most of the organs contained with in it were replaced by a series of roughly equivalent mechanical substitutes. His kneecaps and most of the bones and muscles in his legs were swapped with metal replicas forged from castes of the original parts. Again, after some time, his skin had grown over the metal prosthetics, giving him the appearance of a normal man. No one was exactly sure *why* the

Manazonian government spent so much time and money keeping Tom alive, but rumor had it that his long-time relationship with Company Co-director Rodman Ryder had something to do with it.

"You know, Jerry...if I could save your life....with robot parts or something...I would do it...," said Conrad to Jerry as he thought about Tom's expensive surgeries and the rumors that they had been paid for by his father.

Conrad and Jerry lay there, bound in the sand, beneath the scorching sun. A massive, molting bird with a human arm growing out of its head, like a unicorn horn, circled them, every so often, opening its fanged mouth to let out a screeching *caaaw*!

"Thank you, Conrad," murmured Jerry morosely, between deep, haggard breaths. "That's probably the nicest thing that anyone's ever said to me."

The monstrous bird circling overhead let out another shrill *caaaw* and dropped lower.

"Jerry, *Conrad!*" a deep voice boomed.

Conrad sat bolt upright to identify the source of the voice. Tom was walking toward them. His face was bloody, and his left eye socket was stuffed with densely packed gauze. The right eye socket had a large metal prosthetic eye shoved into it, the pupil of which was an occasionally flashing red LED light. Massive chunks of his skin were missing, revealing the blood caked surface of his metal interior, and when he moved, the gory shredded skin made a sick sticky slurping noise as it slapped against a now bare metal endoskeleton.

"Tom?" Conrad whispered in disbelief, and then, he called out to Tom, struggling against the ropes that bound his arms. "Tom! You're alive. Help! You have to help us! Jerry's dying!"

Tom ran up to the place where they lay, quickly and wordlessly removing a knife from a loop on his belt and cutting the ropes that bound Conrad and Jerry's arms and legs. Tom was carrying a sack over his shoulder, which he dropped on the ground, and started routing through.

"You found the car?" Conrad muttered in

a tone of impressed disbelief.

Tom withdrew a roll of gauze from the bag and handed it to Conrad.

"Put some pressure on that wound before he bleeds out," Tom instructed.

Conrad wasted no time kneeling down next to Jerry and pushing the roll of gauze down onto his dripping wound. The white fabric turned red quickly but Conrad kept pressing down on it.

"I had a GPS tracker installed in my wrist a few years ago," Tom explained. "I had put a receiver chip on the car and both of you guys before we came out here incase we got separated."

"*What?*" Conrad grumbled, somehow

finding the nerve to be insulted by this.

"Yea, your dad was pretty insistent that I keep track of you," said Tom. "So he put a tracker chip on the inside of your shirt."

"That. *Shit*," Conrad swore, at a loss for words. As grateful as he was to still be alive, he still did not much like the idea that his dad thought of him as a baby that needed to be kept track of.

The monstrous bird overhead head cawed again, and then, swooped down. Conrad ducked to avoid being speared by its talons, which were as large and as sharp as javelins.

"*Run!*" Tom yelled, and he sprinted off into the distance, still carrying the sack.

Conrad grabbed Jerry and through him

over his shoulder, then, began to run as well. The bird dropped low in the sky and began racing after them. The monster was much, much larger than it had appeared in the air; and really, much more like a dragon than a bird.

Conrad and Tom ran, struggling to move as their heavy feet sunk low in the yellow sand. The massive bird was approaching quickly. There was a rock formation in the distance. It looked like there was a small, hollow opening in its base, a few hundred feet away. Conrad and Tom instinctually ran towards it. It was a place to hide where the vast bird monster would not be able to follow. The creature's massive wingspan would simply not allow it.

Conrad and Tom ran, the distant rock

formation growing closer and closer with every passing second. The monster bird shot up into the sky and accelerated. Then, it swooped down and grabbed a screaming Tom in its massive talons. It shot back up into the air with Tom's bloody shredded body thrashing in its tight grip. The sack of supplies slipped out of Tom's flailing arms and fell back down into the sand.

The monstrous bird flew off into the distance, disappearing from sight, and, as it did so, Tom's screams faded to silence.

10

Conrad doubled back and grabbed the sack of supplies with his free hand, then, turned back around and started running toward the rock formation again. Jerry was limp in

Conrad's arms, and the blood from his dripping body seeped through Conrad's white shirt, staining it red.

"Are you, ok?" Conrad asked Jerry stupidly as he grew closer to the rock formation.

Jerry did not respond.

"Hey, you're gonna to be fine," said Conrad as much for his own benefit as for Jerry's.

The rock formation, now a mere five or six feet in front of them, was a tall, jagged structure made of yellowish-brown, sand-colored stone. It was tall and narrow, and there were many holes in it, that may have once been the burrows of a freight train-sized subterranean worm.

Conrad entered an arch-shaped hole at the base of the rock formation. In many places the stone structure had been corroded smooth. The walls and floors here were the texture of polished marble and in places they reflected the light of the glaring sun, which shone through the network of tunnels overhead.

Conrad laid Jerry's body down in a place where the sand gave way to smooth yellowish-brown stone, under the shade of a jagged arch. He then dumped the contents of Tom's sack of supplies onto the ground. Tom had thought to save a few dozen cans of food, bottles of water, disinfectant, gauze, and medical supplies.

Jerry was still. His eyes were unfocused and he was unresponsive, but his chest was still heaving ever so slightly. And Conrad, seeing that the man was still alive, crouched down by his side, reached his large hands out and unbuttoned the top button of Jerry's bloody button down shirt.

Jerry's eyes shot open, and his hand flew to Conrad's, as he attempted weakly to pry the larger man off of his shirt.

"Conrad, *stop*," Jerry murmured weakly. "You have to let me die."

Conrad shook his head and pulled Jerry's hands away from the bloody button down shirt. *He can't know what he's saying*, Conrad thought frantically. *He has to be delusional from blood loss.* Quickly, Conrad unbuttoned the shirt. There was a second piece of fabric underneath: a bloody, tight, white stretch of fabric, which covered Jerry's upper body above the belly button and below the collar bone. Conrad grabbed a pocket knife from the pile of supplies and with one, swift, frantic motion, sliced the undershirt down the middle so that it fell open.

Conrad's eyes grew wide and his chest began to heave faster as he was overtaken by a spasm of panic-stricken hyperventilating. He felt tears prick the corners of his eyes.

"No," he whispered, shaking his head. "*No*...it can't be."

There was a bloody, seeping hole in Jerry's chest and, below that, a pair of small, round protrusions surrounding the nipples. These were, without a doubt, the shman deformities.

"Let me die, Conrad," Jerry whispered weakly, his (her?) voice as cold and emotionless as a digital voice recording on a pull string doll. "…This is the way it should be."

Conrad stood up and took a step backward, breathing heavily. He drew a large hand back through his blond bangs, wiping sweat from his sunburned forehead, and blinked back tears. Then, he dropped to his knees in the sand next to where Jerry's body lay, closing his eyes and raising the pocket knife high, prepared to deliver the death blow.

How could the monster he had been hunting have been hiding right in front of him this entire time? Conrad took a deep rattling breath, and raised the knife higher, procrastinating. Every memory he had of Jerry came flooding back to him in that instant, his shrill laugh, the glare reflecting off of those thick glasses as Conrad's red convertible raced forward, blowing back his short auburn hair. Conrad pushed the thought away and willed himself to feel nothing. *This is not a man,* Conrad reminded himself. *It's only a monster that looks like a man. It doesn't feel. It only pretends that it can, to keep its self alive...the way an animal does.* Conrad took another deep breath and opened his eyes. Jerry stared up at the ceiling, his eyes unfocused, the heaving of his lumpy chest slowing with every passing second. A disturbing thought cross Conrad's mind: *but what if that's not true.* The image of Jerry forced itself back into Conrad's mind. He was sitting at the kitchen table in his apartment, cleaning his gun, and the Testosterone Tyrone marathon was glaring in the background. He stopped to adjust her glasses and grin at Conrad, who was sitting across from him.

"You know, Conrad," he said. "You're really not as bad as I thought you were." He picked the gun back up and started cleaning it again. In the background, Testosterone Tyrone threw a grenade and the resulting explosion echoed throughout the apartment. "I'm kind of glad I got to know the real you."

Conrad inhaled deeply, and then, threw the knife across the cave so that it hit one of the stone walls and bounced off, clattering on to the ground. He let a out a slow, shuttering sob, and then, overcome with a barrage of powerful and confusing emotions, began to weep loudly and frantically. He grabbed the gauze and the disinfectant from the pile of supplies, and got to work, quickly and carefully dressing Jerry's wound, continuing to weep as he did so.

When he was finished, remembering that his father had put a tracking device inside of his shirt, he removed the shirt, wiped the tears and snot off of his face with it, and threw it on the ground. Then, he found a lighter in the pile of supplies, clicked it on, and burned the shirt to ash.

11

That night, Conrad dreamed of Lucy. She was standing on the bridge in Manazonia Central Park, her long, sunflower yellow hair caught in a spectral breeze as she walked slowly over the bridge. She had her back turned toward Conrad, and he walked slowly closer to her, fearful that she would notice him and run away.

It must have been Autumn because the surrounding trees were orange, red, yellow, and brown with the promise of their impending decay. The leaves moved in the wind and the bright sunlight overhead cast a tie-dye of orange glow across each branch's rippling surface.

Lucy stopped walking when she reach the

center of the bridge, and put her hands on the railing. Conrad watched her as she stared out at the rustling Autumn leaves. She was wearing a long, bubble gum pink skirt, trimmed in white lace, and she carried a pink camisole, which obscured her face from Conrad's line of vision.

"Lucy!" Conrad shouted and he bounded over to her.

Lucy turned away from him and continued to walk.

"Lucy...Lucy, *Wait!*" Conrad shouted, and he sprinted to catch up with her, reached out, grabbed one of her shoulders and spun her around.

As she turned, her long, wavy locks shifted from blond to dark auburn. They spun around her in slow motion and a few Autumn leaves drifted slowly past her bewildered face. She had large, thick-framed glasses, that caught the light of the bright sun and reflected it back for a moment, temporarily obscuring her eyes. Beneath, was a homely, androgynous face, painted to look garishly feminine. Despite the paint, however, she was unmistakably Jerry.

"Conrad?" Jerry murmured confusedly, lowering her umbrella.

Overcome with a sudden and overpowering affection for her, Conrad extended his arms and embraced her, enjoying the warmth of her small body against his bare chest.

He opened his eyes slowly and saw the

real Jerry lying asleep in the sand in front of him. He must have rolled over and put his arm around the smaller man some time during the night because Jerry's back was pressed against Conrad's bare chest and Conrad's fingers where clutching Jerry's stained bandages. Conrad let out a sigh that was symptom of both contentment and creeping anxiety, and then, closed his eyes and went back to sleep.

Days passed. Jerry slept a lot and did not speak to Conrad much. On the rare occasions that Jerry *did* speak, it was only to suggest in a pissed-off voice that Conrad complete the mission and kill him.

"Why are you suicidal all of a sudden?" Conrad asked one day, and he was surprised to hear Jerry answer him. Jerry had not responded to anything that Conrad had said directly, since the night that he had discovered that Jerry possessed female anatomy.

"I've always been suicidal. Why do you think I became a Company Man?"

Conrad sat down in the sand next to him. For the last week or so, Conrad had spent his days wandering lost in the desert, hunting strange lands beasts, and his nights, cooking them over an open fire. The idea that Jerry would still want to die after he had put so much time and effort into keeping Jerry alive concerned him. Especially since he had been wearing a bug that included a direct audio and visual feed to Manazonia at the moment that he had discovered that Jerry was female. There was a good chance that the Manazonian government knew about Jerry and there was a good chance that they knew Conrad was helping him as well. By continuing to keep Jerry alive, Conrad was essentially sacrificing everything he had ever known. He could never again return to Manazonia, for fear of death, torture, or imprisonment in a mental institution.

"Don't throw your life away, Conrad," Jerry said coldly. "You can still kill me and bring my corpse back with you to Manazonia. You'll be welcomed as a hero. Finish the job."

"I can't...," said Conrad.

"I'm a monster, Conrad. Be a man and finish the job," Jerry seethed, irritated by

Conrad's noncompliance and the cold fearless urgency of the statement hit Conrad in the gut like a fist.

Conrad felt tears well up behind his eyes and blinked them back.

"I...I don't care if you *are* a monster!" he blurted out stupidly. "I'm *never* letting you die!"

The two were quiet for a moment. Outside the rock formation, the sun sank low in the sky. Mutant crickets chirped, spewing green slime from their boil-covered thoraxes as they did so.

"There's a lot of monsters out here, Conrad," said Jerry quietly. "Why don't you just go be friends with *one of them* and *leave me alone*?"

"Do you know who is more negative about everything ever than even *you* are?" Conrad asked.

"Who?"

"My *nut sack*."

"Great. Go be friends with your nut sack. Draw a little face on it with magic marker. You'll get by," said Jerry.

Outside, the mutant crickets chirped. The sun sank lower in the sky, bathing The Strange Lands in a bright yellowish-orange glow.

"Hey, Jerry," Conrad asked quietly.

"Yea?"

"Since you're Lucy..."

"I'm not *Lucy*," Jerry said. "Lucy is just a legend. I'm *me*."

"But you *are* a…a…*she*?"

"I'm a *he*, Conrad. I'm *not* a woman. I mean…technically I guess I am a woman, but, damn it, I'm still *a Manazonian*. I don't want you to think about me as one of those…those *things*…I'm just a normal guy. I'm just the same guy I've always been."

"Oh…ok. But I'm kind of curious about something," said Conrad.

"Conrad, I'm not showing you my genitals," said Jerry humorlessly.

"It's not that…I mean well…it is that…but um…also….how did you become a shman?" Conrad asked uncomfortably.

"I didn't *become* a shman," said Jerry. "I was born this way. The birthing factory must have glitched and circumcised a male infant in my place, then delivered me to my fathers instead, just like Weston said. One of my fathers was really sick and on his death bed around the time that I was born, and he died when I was little. So my dad, he must have been really lonely. Which, is why, I think, he kept my deformities a secret. He couldn't take having to give up his son on top of that."

The sun disappeared under the horizon and darkness came. A mutant owl with two heads and dozens of grotesque vestigial legs protruding from its body landed softly on a cactus flower and hooted.

Jerry continued his story: "For the longest time, I didn't know what I was. I only knew that

I was different. But not in a good way. I was always small for my age and I was never as strong or as fast as the other kids. Then, when I was about thirteen, I started getting painful bleeding out of the hole in my crotch."

"*Eww...*" Conrad shuttered.

"Conrad, shut up. I'm telling a story," said Jerry, and then, he continued: "My dad thought it must have been because I was dying, and that my deformities were ultimately fatal ones. So I got used to the idea that I was probably going to die young. Then, around high school, when all of the other boys were getting bigger and stronger and more handsome, I started growing these awful goiters on my chest instead. My dad showed me how to hide them with binding and a compression shirt, but they were still, you know. *There.* God, I hated them. I still hate them. A couple times I actually thought about trying to saw them off."

"Did it work?" Conrad asked.

"No, Conrad. It didn't *work*. What do you think they *grew back*?"

"I don't know," said Conrad, shrugging. "*Do* they grow back?"

Jerry shook his head.

"Um... I was never actually able to saw them off, so yea...I guess the actual answer to your question is...I have *no* clue. Are they cancer? Did some mosquitoes lay eggs under my skin? Are they going to hatch into giant, squishy parasites? I don't fucking know. They haven't yet. That's all *I* know. Anyway, back to the story. So I was in high school, right, and I was failing gym class because my stupid noodle arms can't do one pull-up. When I start to notice that my hips are getting ridiculous. I mean, my fat distribution was disturbing. I was monstrously ugly. I mean, it didn't really matter because I could never have a boyfriend anyway, they would have found out what was wrong with me and told the government. But still I wanted to look normal. Looking normal was a lot of work but eventually I got the hang of it.

Conrad laid down in the sand next to Jerry and stared up at the ceiling of the rock formation overhead. He tried to picture what Jerry had looked like before he looked "normal."

"So now, I'm studying all the time so that I can still graduate with a failing grade in gym class, but, at the same time, I'm eating a lot less just so that I can look normal. I am under so much stress that, one day, I just don't go to school, and, instead, I just go to a movie theater and wander around all day, sneaking into shows," Jerry said. He paused and sat up, staring off into the distance. "I was 17 when the first Testosterone Tyrone movie came out....and when I saw it...I ....I don't know, it just stuck with me. It was Tyrone, I think. I wanted to be with him but also...I wanted to *be* him. It was a whole complicated *thing*. He was everything that I wasn't."

Jerry laid back down in the sand and

stared up at the ceiling of the rock formation.

"Tyrone was strong, you know. He could beat anybody in a fight. It didn't matter if both of his hands were trapped in a triple helix bullshit vortex from Mars, and his a opponent was 20 feet tall, with giant laser magnetron sharks shooting out of his eyes. He still always won. He was indestructible, you know. A *real* man. But, then, he wasn't just any man, was he? He was a *Company* Man."

"He's not just aaaany man. He's a Cooompany Man," Conrad sang back at Jerry instinctually. It was impossible not to think of the theme song when he heard the phrase.

"For the first time in my life, I had a goal. A purpose. I knew what I wanted to be," said

Jerry. "So I trained a lot. I still wasn't very fast or strong compared with other kids my age, but I was just fast and strong enough to get by, and my grades were good, so The Company accepted me into their training program. Later, they gave me a job as a criminal sketch artist. And that's about where I was when you met me. They had just promoted me to field work. But the weird thing was, by that point, I was kind of just happy doing criminal sketches. I had matured, you know; accepted my limitations. And you were so..."

"Handsome? Tall? Well groomed?" Conrad offered as the possible second half of Jerry's unfinished sentence.

"*Irritating*," Jerry finished. "I *dreaded*

having to work with you….but I don't know, I guess, after spending a lot of time with you, I came to see you in a different way. I suppose, I have thought about what it might be like…to…to touch you in an intimate way. But then you would have seen what I was…and that would have spelled the end for me. Besides…I don't even have a penis. So how…how…would I….," Jerry sighed. "I don't know….You probably think I'm hideous anyway."

"I think," said Conrad, smiling. "That you're a handsome uh….whatever you are."

"Thanks, Conrad," said Jerry. "I think."

Conrad rolled over on his side and looked at Jerry, laying next to him in the sand. Jerry turned his head and stared back, the spider web cracks in his glasses, obscuring his eyes from view. Conrad reached out and pulled the broken glasses off, folding them carefully, and then, sticking them in one of the pockets of his pants. Underneath, Jerry's eyes were brown and unusually large. Jerry frowned pensively and blinked a few times.

"Everything's blurry all the time now," he said.

"When you heard about Lucy, hiding out in the desert....You must have thought that she was real woman, just like I did," said Conrad.

"Yea," conceded Jerry. "I thought that maybe there were two."

"And you were prepared to kill it, thinking it was...*you know*....like you?"

"Why should I care about other women just because I technically am a woman? I don't care about other women." said Jerry bluntly, putting his head back down in the sand and staring up at the ceiling. "I'd blow up a whole freight car full of 'em, if it would in someway benefit me."

Conrad laughed. It was a deep throaty laugh that made his Addam's apple quiver in his thick neck. He smiled big, revealing many of his big, square, white teeth.

"I guess I would too," he conceded.

The mutant owl outside hooted and took off into the sky. Under the light of the red moon, it looked like something demonic. Curiosity got the better of Conrad, and he imagined what it might be like to make love to a humanoid monster with goiters growing out of its chest and blood squirting out of its alien crotch hole. This was his chance to find out, once and for all, what that was like. This was his chance to explore the experimental erotic terror of mounting a mythical beast of legend. He decided to make his move.

"Hey, Jerry?"

"Yea?"

"Can I kiss you?"

Jerry rolled over onto his side and pressed his body into Conrad, his face brushing against his.

"You know what, Conrad," he murmured quietly. "You earned it."

Conrad moved his head closer to Jerry's, pressed his lips against Jerry's, and opened his mouth, sliding his tongue between Jerry's lips. Jerry closed his eyes. He had never been kissed before, but could tell by the way that Conrad moved his tongue that he had practiced this many, *many* times.

Jerry pulled away and wiped some saliva off of his lips with the back of his hand.

"Conrad?"

"Yea?"

"If I tell you something kinda gross, can you promise not to get grossed out?" Jerry asked.

"Buddy, it takes *a lot* to gross *me* out," said Conrad proudly.

"Hm...good to know. Well um...I...I sometimes wonder what it would be like...to um...to..."

"To *what*?" Conrad asked, a bit irritated by Jerry's hesitance.

Jerry put his lips close to Conrad's ear and whispered something.

Conrad grinned.

"That can be arranged," he said.

Then, Conrad thought about something and the grin slipped off his face.

"But it's not lined with spikes, is it?" Conrad asked with some concern. The thought had not crossed his mind at times when he had thought that sticking his penis in a shman's crotch hole was only an impossible fantasy.

Jerry Shrugged.

"I dunno," he said.

"Does it squirt corrosive acid?" Conrad asked.

"I *dunno*," Jerry said, shrugging again.

Conrad leaned into Jerry and kissed him again, pushing away his fears of the unknown. Jerry wanted this. Jerry needed to feel like he was attractive. Jerry needed to feel like he was a real man. Conrad was going to do this for his tiny, deformed friend. A disturbing thought crossed Conrad's mind and he broke the kiss.

"There aren't uh…parasitic worms up in there…that'll crawl into my penis? Are there?" he asked, voicing his new concern.

Jerry shrugged again.

"To fuck if I know," Jerry said, with some irritation, and then, he lunged forward and began kissing Conrad's partially open, bewildered mouth, with sloppy virgin tongue.

Outside, the stars shined brightly. The red moon was round and vast, like the glowing eye of a demonic beast. It seemed to peer at them through the darkness, casting an eerie glow that tinged the sand crimson with the promise of impending discord.

12

There was a harsh, abrupt knock on the door. Jerry's father flinched and looked up from his newspaper. The German Sheppard, Dionysus, jumped off his lap and bolted toward the source of the noise, howling madly.

"Is this the residence of Jerry Cosco Senior?" a deep, threatening voice demanded from the other side of the door.

Jerry's father stood up and walked over to the door, unlocking the dead bolt with a shaking hand. Then, he opened the door. A fleet of ten or twenty heavily-armed Company Men, in dark blue uniforms, were standing there.

"Uh...yes it is," the old man answered timidly, his bony hands gripping the newspaper tightly. "Please. Come in."

The Company Men spilled into the room like water, dispersing so that there was a tall, heavily-armed man everywhere Jerry's father looked. Dionysus ran frantic circles around their legs barking and panting and wagging his tail.

———

The crowd of Company Men parted as Churchill strolled up to Jerry's father, his expression blank, unreadable. The man wore a long black coat over his company uniform and walked slowly, as though taking a leisurely stroll through the park. The dog bounded over to him, and he removed his hands from the pockets of his coat to pet the dog's head until his panting slowed, and he was calm. Then, Churchill straightened up and readjusted his black fedora. The dog remained at his feet, staring up at the man with a look of ignorant, doglike admiration.

"I'll be frank with you, Mr. Cosco," said Churchill coldly. "We know that you've been hiding the monster."

"The monster?" Jerry's father replied, trying to sound confused. Sweat pricked his brow and he swallowed hard. "What in the world are you talking about, Churchill?"

"We have reason to believe that your son, Jerry Cosco Jr., was born with the shman deformities," Churchill elaborated. "And that instead of returning her to the birthing factory to be humanely euthanized, you kept the monster's existence a secret from the government...for *twenty one years*."

"That's....that's the most insane accusation I've ever heard," stuttered Jerry's father. He stood up and stared Churchill in the eye defiantly. "If Jerry is a shman, then how was he smart enough to learn English? How is it that he can read and write and feed himself?"

"Not my concern," said Churchill dismissively.

"Jerry has worked for the company for years," argued Jerry's father. "If he was a shman, don't you think someone would have noticed it by now? If he was a shman, would he have even made it through the training program?"

"Yes, well, you can train a parrot to recite the laws of physics but that doesn't make him Isaac Newton, does it?" replied Churchill. "We have evidence that she is, in fact, a shman."

"I want to see my lawyer," Jerry's father said.

Churchill shook his head.

"There's no need for that," he said. "We have video evidence that you are lying. We have also raided Jerry's apartment and found compression shirts. There were no razors, shaving cream or shaving related items found anywhere, suggesting that perhaps Jerry has never grown a beard. However, all of this is inconsequential, Mr. Cosco, because you have already been found guilty in the court of The Overlords. Their verdict is final. The penalty for your transgression, will be death."

All of the Company Men in the room removed their guns from the loops on their belts and pointed them at Jerry's father. Churchill knelt down and attached a leash to Dionysus. He then turned and walked from the room, dragging the thrashing snarling dog behind him.

"Now's your chance to repent, Mr. Cosco. Make your peace with god." Churchill said as he exited the apartment with the dog, pulling the door closed behind him with a soft *click*.

"I'm not ashamed of what I did, do you hear me!" Jerry's father yelled after the now absent Churchill. Tears began to roll down his wrinkled face. "The Company Men took *everything* from me! My brother, my career, my future, my Darrel, *Everything*!...But I wasn't about to let them take *my son*! Never *my son*!"

The command to kill was muttered by Churchill and received through the ear pieces of each Company Man in the room. A barrage of gunshots rang out, as they all unloaded their clips into Jerry's father's head and chest. Jerry's father fell to his knees. His blood was bright and red under the room's white fluorescent ceiling light. It gushed from his body, spilling over him in red waterfalls as he dropped to his knees. Then, he fell forward into the carpet, dead.

<u>13</u>

After four months of hiding out in The Strange Lands, Conrad's beard had grown long and his skin had grown dark. Foraging for food was now second nature to him. As he had run out of bullets and explosives long ago and now had to use only his physical strength and his knives to make kills. He learned quickly that, with this limitation, it was smarter to hunt small animals and run from big ones.

During the day, Conrad chased mutant rats, penis scorpions and three-eyed desert toads by jumping on them and slitting their throats or crushing them dead with his bare hands. During the night he returned to Jerry, who had contracted, what, by his estimation, must have been some kind of a mysterious and possibly fatal Strange Lands illness. Jerry spent his days vomiting and laying ill under the shade of the stone overhang. His belly had grown large and bloated, with what was probably a growing tangle of wiggling parasites. Sometimes Conrad felt them wriggle and push against him through the smaller man's skin when he was laying next to Jerry at night. It made him think that his companion must not have had much more time left to live.

One day, when Conrad was out hunting and foraging. He spotted a black armored car emblazoned with the insignia of The Company. He hid in the shadow of a large cactus and watched it drive into the distance and disappear from sight. *Damn*, Conrad thought. *We're being hunted by Company Men, aren't we? Looks like they're close to figuring out where we are too.*

That night, Conrad and Jerry left the rock formation that had been their shade and their shelter for months. They walked for a long time. A mutant owl hooted softly in the distance. Crickets chirped, desert toads croaked, a two-headed vulture with a slimy arc of human arms growing down its back bellowed an unholy *crrraaaaaaaaaaaaaa.*

After some time, they reached a bizarre metal building that was painted to look like a sandy-colored rock formation. There was a metal door on the side of the building. And, on the metal door, there was a square, white, laminated sign, with the following words printed on it:

"No Trespassing! This is an Overlords' Residence!"

Jerry stared at the sign for a moment, confused.

"An Overlords' Residence? What does *that* mean?" he whispered.

"Maybe...the Overlords live here? They have to live somewhere right?" said Conrad.

"Come on. Let's get out of here."

Jerry stared at the sign on the door for another moment.

"No," he said quietly. "My belly parasites are going to kill me soon. I want to see The Overlords before I die. You go ahead without me."

"Jerry…the life you have left…it's precious."

"Living, knowing that you haven't got much longer to live, is no kind of life," said Jerry coldly.

Then, the two-headed vulture swooped down on them, as it shrieked its earsplitting caw. To avoid being grabbed by its razor sharp talons, Jerry and Conrad pushed the door to the building open and ran inside.

Jerry and Conrad glanced around. They were now inside of a tall, long, metal room, covered in computer monitors and control panels. A few men in white lab coats wandered around, watching the monitors, taking notes, turning knobs, and pushing buttons.

A younger man with short dark hair and a pair of large glasses, glanced away from his control panel to take a look at Jerry and Conrad, who were both sunburned and ragged with long wild tangles of matted hair.

"Uh...sir? We have visitors," the young man with the dark hair said.

A gangly, nebbish man in his forties with short, graying sandy blood hair and a pair of square wire framed glasses, rose from a computer chair in front of the largest central monitor. He walked over to them, grinning, hands in the pockets of his white lab coat.

"You must be the Manazonians," the man said, walking over to Jerry. Conrad stepped in front of him and glowered dangerously, blocking the mysterious man's path.

"You don't have to fear me. I'm only an objective observer," the man said, and then, he removed his hands from the pockets of his lab coat both to show Conrad that he was holding no weapons and to point to himself with both of them. "Dr. Thomas Edwards."

"Who?" Conrad asked.

"You Manazonians know me as Overlord

Alpha," said Edwards. "But really I'm the director of the Manazonia project."

"The *what*?" Jerry murmured with disbelief. "What's *that*?"

Edwards snickered and a few of the other lab coated men did so as well.

"God I love, Tell a Strange Lands resident the truth day. It's the best day of the year," Edwards said. "You have no idea, Jerry. This holiday I've invented...it's better than Christmas. You should see the look on your face."

"I don't understand," said Jerry.

"What do you two believe about The Strange Lands?" Edwards asked.

"The Strange Lands....covers the entire

planet surrounding Manazonia. It was reduced to desert by nuclear war, and the nuclear fallout created The Strange Lands beasts," said Jerry.

"Yea, what he said," said Conrad.

"Wrong," said Edwards. "The Strange Lands is only a desert with a tall, barbed wire fence around it. At its center is a thing called The Biotech Company, where this planet's best trained and most respected scientists make new technology for a variety of lucrative markets. Surrounding The Biotech Company, is Biotech City where the scientists and their families live. And surrounding Biotech City, is the desert, which serves a variety of our purposes. The first being secrecy. We can't have liberal groups halt our projects with their ridiculous notions of ethics. The desert's second purpose, we dump our test animals and failed experiments there. Why, you might ask? The answer: Fast and humane disposal. Cheap, easy clean up. Plus the hazardous little ecosystem we've created by simply releasing our abominations keeps our thought experiments in their ideal isolated states."

"Are you going to talk for much longer? This is starting to feel like homework," grumbled Conrad impatiently.

"Shut up, Conrad. I'm trying to rock your world view," said Edwards, and then, he continued monologueing as though he hadn't been interrupted. "What is a thought experiment, you might ask? Well I'm glad you might ask that, Manazonians, because I might definitely tell you."

"You tell 'em, boss!" one of the lab coated men, called from his chair in front of a complicated-looking control panel. Then, he flipped a few switches on the control panel and looked back down at what he was doing.

"Thought experiments," said Edwards. "Are colonies manufactured by The Biotech Company. The population of each one was grown from a collection of volunteers who signed away their rights for a check and became our guinea pigs. Their brains were altered to forget the real world and remember the histories we invented. In this way, we were able to create a variety of self-contained societies, each with its own manufactured eccentricities. Each serves as a fascinating social experiment, as social science was a hobby of Biotech Company's original founder. The social science component of thought experiment colonies continues to this day. However, the colonies serve the *major* function of providing our company with limitless guinea pigs. Our many thought experiments are all mostly self sufficient now and the perfect test settings for products, diseases, and market research."

"Of course, Manazonia had existed for years and years before I came to work here, and was later promoted to my position of Director of the Manazonia project. But still, damn, right? Who knew that a gay kid from North Dakota could make it so far?"

"What's gay?" asked Conrad.

"What's North Dakota?" asked Jerry.

Edwards shook his head.

"Not relevant," he said. "I better stop talking before your little Manazonian brains explode."

"Aww…that's no fun, boss!" one of the lab coated men called out as he flipped a few switches on his control panel.

"Is this Tell a Strange Lands resident the Truth Day or isn't it?" another of the lab coated men called out.

Edwards sighed and shook his head again.

"Yea, I guess it is," Edwards conceded.

"The truth is that I'm telling you all of these things because I'd like to help you. I've been watching you both for a long time and by now, I have to say, I really rather sympathize with your plight. As an employee of The Biotech Company, I am supposed to be an impartial observer in all this and not interfere in the lives of the Manazonians more than I strictly have to. But, I suppose, I've never followed that rule before, have I? Why should I start now? It's not like my boss will ever know about this."

Edward sighed deeply, and then, continued in a much more serious voice: "Jerry, Conrad, outside of the Strange Lands, there's a whole big, wide, world filled with biological men who live in communities with biological woman, and don't murder them. Well...most of the time. There, Jerry can live in peace without being hunted down by the government. Head south until you reach the outer barrier. You'll get there."

"I don't believe you," said Jerry.

"What was that, I wasn't paying attention to anything you just said for awhile," said Conrad. He had grown board by Edwards' nonsensical, probably made up, explanation of their world and was now looking around the room instead.

"Well, I've done all I can do. My boss is...how should I put this....a *real* scary man. So, *yea*...I'm not going to interfere anymore than I already have," said Edwards, shrugging.

"Proof," said Jerry quietly, his large, brown eyes glued to Edwards' weirdly magnified blue ones. "I want proof that the world you're talking about really exists. If you're really trying to help us, we'll need some proof before we risk our lives walking all the way to the edge of something....*that might not even have an edge.*"

"Uh...um...," Edwards muttered, scratching his head. "Well there really aren't that many women working for The Biotech Company, none in this particular control room, anyway...so uh...."

"Convenient. I want to see proof," said Jerry.

"Yea, what he said," agreed Conrad

rather dispassionately. He really wasn't paying attention to what they were saying. Instead, he was watching the screens that lined the walls with quiet awe. City streets bustling with Manazonians, birthing factory workers sorting infants into metal boxes, and top secret government meetings were being broadcasted before his eyes.

"Uh...right. I know," said Edwards brightly, after some contemplation. He walked over to a stretch of metal wall uncovered by screens and control panels. Here there was a framed photograph of a graduating class. "It's not much in the way of proof, but perhaps it will inspire you to take that leap of faith. *Look*."

Jerry stared at the photograph. A

bleacher filled with smiling men in white and yellow graduate gowns stared back. Conrad walked over to them and looked at the photograph as well, perhaps expecting more porn.

"It's just a picture of a bunch of men in graduate costumes," said Jerry. He could see what was clearly the younger version of Edwards, standing near the bottom right corner of the photograph. To his left was a man with large glasses, a bristly unshaven face and dark, shaggy hair. To his right was a pudgy fellow with a prematurely receding hairline. There was nothing here to suggest that the world Edwards was talking about, where men and women live together, actually existed.

"Look closer," said Edwards, smiling. "One of these things is not like the other."

Jerry and Conrad stared at the photograph for awhile and Edwards grinned, amused by their ignorance. A few long moments passed. Jerry and Conrad continued to stare at the photograph, searching for something that could be counted as proof that Edwards was not lying to them. After some time , the smirk slipped off of Edwards' face, and, frustrated by Jerry and Conrad's inability to pick out the woman, he pointed to her and blurted out: "It's her. She's a woman. She has breasts. She has hips. She's a woman. She may not be a *pretty* woman but, damn it, she's a woman."

"Speak for yourself, boss, Slicer is *hot*,"

said one of the younger scientists as he walked by, holding a cardboard box that was overflowing with miscellaneous machine parts.

Jerry and Conrad stared at the person that Edwards was pointing to in the photograph. The alleged female was standing to the left of the man with the bristly face and shaggy dark hair, in the extreme right bottom corner of the photograph. She was short and her graduate gown was less white and more yellow than the gowns of the men who surrounded her. Her face was plain and unpainted and she wore large, thick framed angular glasses, but despite this, even the Manazonians could tell that she definitely was a woman. She was curvy and large-breasted with long, straight brown hair pulled into a sideways ponytail.

"Oh ok. I see it now," said Conrad. "He's a shman."

"She can't be," said Jerry with disbelief.

"She is," said Edwards, smiling. "This is my dear friend, Maurine Slicer. She was the only woman to graduate from Biotech University in the same year that I did, and part of my crew, back in the day. Slicer was really a remarkable woman. She spoke six different languages, tested with an IQ well above average and graduated at the top of the class. But despite all that, she wasn't stuffy and boring like you would think. A bit conceded maybe. Not boring. Nobody was more fun to science with than Maurine Slicer. Nobody," Edwards put the photo back on the wall and chuckled sinisterly as he continued to smile fondly, remembering the woman. "It was Slicer that taught me my motto. *'Science,*'she would say to me. *'is more important than people.'"*

"You keep talking about her in the past tense, like something happened to her," said Jerry suspiciously.

"Uh...yea," Edwards chuckled nervously. "She's kind of probably dead. Most likely. Slicer lost her mind and ran into the desert screaming a few days after this picture was taken."

Jerry narrowed his eyes with agitation. This was not the "proof" he had been hoping for. Conrad stared at the picture of the woman on the wall with a critical eye. *This picture might have been digitally altered,* he thought.

"But don't let *that* discourage you two. I assure you that there's plenty more women out there than just her," said Edwards.

"Come on, Jerry. Let's get out of here," said Conrad, walking toward the exit. He was eager to leave this bizarre metal building, which may very well have been a trap. He was also eager to end this conversation, which very well may have been a distraction to keep them standing in the trap.

"Thank you for the entertaining story, Mr. Edwards," Jerry said, and then, he followed Conrad to the exit.

"Jerry, wait!" Edwards called after him.

He jogged over to Jerry and Jerry turned back around, staring blankly.

"You look like you could use a new pair of glasses," Edwards said. He reached into one of the pockets of his white lab coat and removed a pair of thick angular glasses, which he then handed to Jerry. Jerry took the glasses out of Edward's hand, removed his broken glasses from his face, and put the glasses that Edwards had handed him on in place of them. He blinked a few times, and then, satisfied that it was better to be dizzy from someone else's prescription, than to put up with the spider web cracks, he said: "Thank you."

"They were Slicer's," said Edwards. "I've been carrying them with me ever since she disappeared. But I think you could use them more than me."

"Uh...thank you," Jerry said again, feeling one of the bizarre angular edges of the glasses with his hand. "But they are a bit weird."

"Yea, sorry," said Edwards. "They're lady's glasses."

Jerry and Conrad exited the metal building quietly. They walked for a while in silence, beneath the intense heat of the relentless son, cutting tracts in the sand with tired, dragging feet. Somewhere in the distance, an unseen monster let out a shrill rattling screech, and the two of them stopped to listen to it as though it were the regaling melody of a colorful and benevolent song bird. Jerry put a hand to his protuberant belly and stared off into the distance, his expression twisted by some profound and incomprehensible emotion.

"Conrad, before I die from this belly parasite," Jerry said quietly, adjusting Slicer's glasses with one bony, sunburned hand. "I want to know whether or not that man was telling the truth."

Conrad leaned into Jerry so that the shadow of his large body shielded the smaller man from the sun.

"Then I guess we better find out," he said.

About the Author:

Coyote Paria is the pen name of an agoraphobic recluse who writes off-beat science fiction and fantasy novels. Coyote also likes drawing, painting, animation, game design, and various nerd stuff.

Other Books by Coyote Paria:

Justice Bitch—
After an accident, billionaire heiress, Harriet Ross, acquires superhuman strength and a psychotic compulsion to brutalize criminals in the name of justice. In order to slake her newly acquired blood lust, Harriet dons a

Justice Bitch Issue 2: Flight of the Poltergeist—
After a furious confrontation, costumed anti-hero, Harriet Ross, is accused of murdering one of the Sexy Rad Super Pals. Harriet believes that the murder was committed by a mysterious superhuman